SAVANNAH'S

VOW

I0679217

BOOK ONE OF
THE HANDLERS
LEGACY

V. R. JOHNSON

ISBN: 979-8-9991999-0-4

To my sister, Anetta Linson — my steadfast light in the darkest nights. Your patience, your sacrifice, and your endless kindness lifted me when I could not stand on my own. You loved me without condition and showed me the true meaning of selfless devotion. I carry your love into every chapter of my life. I pray I will one day give back to you even a fraction of what you have given to me. This story, and every triumph that follows, is because of you.

Table of Contents

ACKNOWLEDGMENTS

Writing Savannah's Vow has been a journey of both heart and endurance. Above all, I thank The Most High for all things. His endless mercy and guidance through every page. I am deeply grateful to my sister, Anetta Linson, whose love and sacrifice made this possible. Thank you to my children Greg, Ryan, Brandon and Alanis who believed in me even when I doubted myself. To those unseen hands — the readers, the dreamers, and the encouragers — this book is for you.

Chapter 1: A New Beginning

The thick Louisiana air clung to Savannah Lacroix as she stepped out of the battered pickup truck and onto the curb at Louis Armstrong New Orleans International Airport. The early morning heat pressed against her skin like a second layer, and the heavy scent of gardenias floated from her grandmother's shawl beside her.

Her fingers tightened around the worn leather handle of her suitcase, her heart pounding faster than the cicadas buzzing in the trees overhead.

Beside her, Grandmother Adéle adjusted her shawl

against the light breeze and pressed something into Savannah's hand - a small, cracked leather journal, the cover worn smooth with age.

"In case you ever need it, chère," her grandmother whispered, her voice thick with a sadness Savannah didn't dare name.

Savannah held the journal tightly, her thumb running over the familiar texture. She could still remember evenings curled at her grandmother's feet, hearing stories about secret things – things half-whispered, half-believed.

A loudspeaker blared the final boarding call for her flight. The sound sliced through Savannah's chest. Tears welled up, but she blinked them back fiercely.

She wrapped her arms around her grandmother, breathing in the familiar smell of gardenias, rosemary, and old paper - the smell of home. She wished, for a wild moment, she could stay wrapped there forever.

"I'll write you," she whispered against her grandmother's shoulder.

"You better," her grandmother said, the softest tremor breaking her voice. "And you listen to your heart, you hear? Not just your head."

Savannah nodded, pulling back reluctantly.

She took one last look as she entered the terminal—her grandmother standing small and proud beside the truck, one hand raised high in farewell, the other clutching a handkerchief she pretended not to need.

The journal was pressed against Savannah's chest like a shield.

It felt, somehow, like she was leaving more than a city behind.

The flight passed in a haze of noise and color.

Savannah barely remembered finding her seat, the polite smiles of the flight attendants, or the rumble of engines as they lifted into the air.

She sat stiffly, forehead against the small, cool window, watching the patchwork of muddy bayous and sprawling fields slip away beneath them.

She thought of nights by the bayou—fireflies winking against the dark, the low croak of frogs, the comforting weight of her grandmother's old quilt wrapped around her legs.

Thought of those books she wasn't supposed to read by flashlight—tales of Egypt, Sumer, forgotten gods, lost empires. Somewhere deep in those ancient stories, she had felt a tug- a whisper promising that the world was larger, stranger, more beautiful and terrible than anyone around her would admit.

She wasn't meant to stay in the small circle of the bayou forever. She had dreams too big for the muddy streets and porch gossip.

At NYU, she would study ancient civilizations, ancient languages, relics from worlds long abandoned. Maybe if she understood enough about the mysteries of the past, she could unlock the ones still haunting her own heart. Maybe she could finally find a place she belonged. Maybe.

She opened the leather journal, just for a moment, running her fingers over the first page. The script was old and careful - winding like river water. Strange phrases. Warnings and riddles – *"Beware the hollow ones who whisper without breath"*. She snapped it closed quickly, heart pounding for reasons she couldn't name. Not yet.

The plane touched down into a gray drizzle, the clouds pressing low over the skyline. Savannah stumbled through the bustling terminal, the chaos of New York hitting her like a wave. People rushed past her in suits and boots, heads down, umbrellas clutched like shields.

She flagged down a yellow cab, the driver giving her a quick once-over before tossing her battered suitcase into the trunk. Inside the cab, she pressed her forehead to the cold glass again, watching the towering skyline rise like a fortress through the mist.

The streets buzzed - horns honking, neon lights flickering even in daylight, vendors shouting from the corners. She caught glimpses of lives rushing by: a woman in red stilettos laughing into her phone, a man pushing a cart stacked high with rainbow umbrellas, a group of students with heavy backpacks huddled under a shared awning.

The air smelled like exhaust, coffee, and something frying—sharp and unfamiliar. It was exhilarating. It was terrifying. It was everything she had hoped for—and nothing like she had imagined.

For one wild, disorienting moment, Savannah wondered if she had made a mistake. But she forced herself to breathe slowly, gripping the journal tighter in her lap. New beginnings never came easy.

The cab pulled up in front of the brownstone on the edge of Greenwich Village—a weathered building with cracked red brick, iron railings tangled with vines, and a small marble plaque reading: Wren House.

It wasn't sleek or modern like the glass towers downtown. It was old, worn at the edges, stubbornly clinging to its own history. Her new home.

Mrs. Patel, a brisk woman with gray hair pulled into a bun so tight it looked painful, met her at the gate. She handed Savannah the keys with little ceremony.

"You're lucky," she said, not unkindly. "Place doesn't stay open long. Private deal. Good price."

Savannah nodded, heart hammering. Somewhere deep inside, a small voice whispered: Ask why. Ask who lived here before. But she shoved the voice away. She didn't want to know. Not yet.

The apartment was small—a single-bedroom nook tucked behind the main staircase—but it had a battered dignity that called to her. The exposed brick walls were faded but beautiful. The wooden floors creaked like a ship rocking on invisible tides. Rain streaked the tall windows, blurring the view of the ancient oak tree outside. The kitchen was little more than a sink, a crooked stove, and a battered fridge, but Savannah smiled anyway. It felt lived-in. It felt real.

When she ran the hot water, the pipes groaned like an old man waking up from a long nap. She signed the lease without hesitation.

That night, Savannah sat cross-legged on the worn wooden floor, a takeout carton of Chinese food balanced on her knees. The noodles were oily and unfamiliar, tasting faintly of sweet soy and something sharp she couldn't place. She swallowed mechanically, missing her grandmother's gumbo—the slow, rich flavor that soaked into your bones, seasoned with patience and love.

The apartment felt too quiet. The rain tapped against the windows politely, like a neighbor who didn't quite know how to introduce themselves. Savannah pulled out the few precious things she had carried across the country: A photo of her parents, frozen in a moment of pure joy. Her mother's small gold cross, worn smooth with time. The cracked leather journal.

She brushed away a tear before it could fall. She wasn't supposed to cry. Not here. Not now.

Savannah fell asleep briefly, sitting against the window, the journal still in her lap. In her dreams, she was small again, barefoot on the porch of her grandmother's house, chasing fireflies through thick summer air. She turned—and for a moment, she thought she saw something shadowy standing at the tree line, watching. When she blinked, it was gone. She woke with a sharp gasp, the room spinning.

The oak tree outside shuddered in the wind, its branches scraping softly against the brick. Savannah pressed her hand against the cold glass, grounding herself. She was here. She was safe.

"I'm really doing this," she whispered, her breath fogging the pane. "I'm really here."

Somewhere in the distance, a siren wailed—sharp and strange. Somewhere closer, footsteps echoed down the hallway beyond her door. The city breathed around her—massive, restless, unknowable. And Savannah Lacroix breathed with it.

She clutched the journal tighter to her chest, remembering her grandmother's words: "You are stronger than you know, chère." And for the first time in a long time, she allowed herself to hope.

Chapter 2: The Coffee Shop Stranger

The distant rumble of delivery trucks and the faint aroma of brewing coffee seeped through Savannah Lacroix's window as the first light of morning crept into her tiny apartment.

She blinked awake slowly, momentarily disoriented, the unfamiliar sounds of the city replacing the soft buzz of cicadas and the rustle of bayou winds she had known all her life.

The mattress beneath her was still bare except for a few crumpled sheets, and a dull ache throbbed between her shoulders—not from any physical strain, but the deep, exhausting weight of heavy emotions.

Still, a small, stubborn smile tugged at her lips. She had made it. Her first night alone in New York City. She stretched, wincing as her muscles protested, and swung her legs onto the creaky floor.

The wood was cold against her bare feet, sending a little shock up her spine. Padding across the room, she rifled through a half-unpacked box, pulling out a pair of jeans, a soft white sweater, and her most reliable boots.

In the bottom of the box, tangled among clothes and papers, her fingers found the delicate gold cross her mother had worn every day. She sat back on her heels for a moment, cradling it in her palm. The chain was thin, the cross simple—but it was the weight of love and memory that made it heavy. Savannah looped it carefully around her neck, pressing the cool metal against her skin for a moment longer before tucking it beneath her sweater.

"I'm still carrying you with me," she whispered.

The city was already wide awake when she stepped outside. A crisp wind tugged at her braid, and the streets were alive with movement—students rushing past with backpacks, vendors shouting over each other as they set up carts, the scent of roasting peanuts mingling with exhaust fumes.

Savannah tightened her jacket around herself and wandered aimlessly, letting the city carry her forward. There was a kind of wild beauty here—not the slow, thick beauty of the bayou, but a restless, pulsing energy. A flower vendor was arranging buckets of damp roses, the petals heavy with dew. An elderly man in a battered tweed cap shuffled by, three tiny dogs in matching sweaters darting around his ankles. Two NYU students zipped past on skateboards, laughing too loudly. Savannah smiled to herself. New York moved faster—harder—but not without charm.

The low brick façade of a café caught her eye, its windows glowing warm against the gray morning. *Hollow & Bean*, the faded letters read above the door. The scent of roasted coffee beans and something buttery and sweet wafted out into the street, wrapping around her like a whispered promise.

Savannah hesitated for a moment, gathering her courage, then pushed open the door. A small brass bell chimed overhead, and for the first time that morning, she felt a sliver of peace.

Inside, the café was a cozy warren of mismatched chairs and narrow tables, lit by hanging Edison bulbs and the flickering glow of a fireplace tucked into one corner. The air buzzed with soft conversation, the clatter of ceramic mugs, the whir of an espresso machine. Savannah soaked it all in—the worn wood floors, the bulletin board cluttered with hand-drawn flyers for poetry readings and indie bands, the scribbled chalkboard menu offering strange delights like flat whites, cortados, and lavender lattes. She joined the line, her stomach fluttering.

This was the kind of place she had dreamed about in the quiet hours back home—a corner of the world where people carved out lives between books and ideas and the steady hum of possibility.

She was studying the menu, trying to decipher the difference between a cortado and a macchiato, when someone bumped lightly into her shoulder.

"Sorry," a deep voice said, rushed but not unfriendly.

Savannah turned, and the world tilted slightly. He stood a few inches taller than most of the crowd, his frame athletic but not bulky. Dark brown hair curled slightly at the edges of his collar, like he had tried to tame it but ultimately let it do as it pleased. He wore a soft gray sweater, jeans, boots worn but clean—simple, effortless. But it was his face that caught her—a strong, chiseled jaw, high cheekbones, and piercing blue-gray eyes that seemed to see straight through the surface of her. For a moment, she forgot how breathing worked.

"No problem," she said, hoping her voice didn't betray the way her heart had just flipped.

He smiled—a real, genuine smile, not the tight, distracted grimace she had already seen so many New Yorkers wear—and it softened his sharpness into something dangerously beautiful. "First time here?" he asked, his voice low and warm.

Savannah laughed, brushing a loose strand of hair behind her ear. "Is it that obvious?"

He leaned in slightly, dropping his voice into a playful, conspiratorial tone. "Only because you're looking at the menu like it personally insulted you."

Savannah grinned, feeling a flush creep into her cheeks. "I was trying to decode it," she admitted.

"Order the lavender latte," he said. "Sounds ridiculous. Tastes like heaven."

Savannah lifted a brow. "I'll take your word for it."

They moved forward in line together, the easy flow of conversation surprising her. It felt... natural. Unforced. Like she was slipping into a conversation that had started long before she walked in.

He ordered a black coffee—no cream, no sugar—while she nervously asked for the lavender latte. When she reached into her pocket for her wallet, he was faster, slipping a twenty across the counter with a smooth flick of his wrist.

"Wait—you didn't have to—" Savannah started.

"I know," he said, flashing another of those devastating smiles. "Welcome to New York." As he handed the cashier a casual wave, Savannah caught a glimpse of something strange. There, inked neatly between the thumb and forefinger of his right hand, was a small tattoo — a stark black number: 1. It was tiny, almost hidden in the play of shadows and warm café light. But it caught her attention. It was strangely compelling. Before she could ask, before she could even properly process it, he was backing away, coffee in hand.

"I'm Jamie," he said, tilting his head slightly.

"Savannah," she managed, the name tasting almost new in her mouth.

"Nice to meet you, Savannah," Jamie said, his voice wrapping around her like velvet. And then—with a nod and a wink that sent another sharp flutter through her chest— he slipped out into the river of commuters flowing past the window. Gone.

Savannah stood there for a moment longer than she

should have, clutching her latte to her chest. The scent of lavender and espresso rose around her in comforting waves, but her heart still hammered against her ribs. She found a corner table and sat down, barely tasting the first sip of her drink.

I didn't even get his number. She laughed softly at herself, shaking her head.

New York—wild, unpredictable, larger than life— had finally reached out and touched her back.

She thought again of the tiny tattoo she had seen— simple, stark, strangely mesmerizing. The number one. Odd. Unforgettable. Maybe she would never see him again.

And yet...

Savannah sat there, the city breathing around her, the rain tapping against the windows, the faint hum of life buzzing through the air. Somewhere deep inside her, something stirred. Not fear. Not even longing. Hope.

Chapter 3: The Girl Next Door

Savannah struggled up the narrow staircase, arms full of grocery bags and her keys dangling precariously from one finger. The ancient wooden steps groaned with every footfall, and the thin carpet runner did little to muffle the sounds of the bustling city leaking through the hall's cracked windows. She huffed out a breath, adjusting the bags that cut into her wrists. Small victories, she thought. Buying groceries, finding her way back without getting hopelessly lost — they were victories all the same. The second-floor landing creaked under her boots just as one of the bags tore open slightly, a box of cereal threatening to tumble free.

"Need a hand?" The voice was bright — musical, but with that unmistakable sharp New York edge.

Savannah turned, startled, and saw a young woman leaning casually against the doorframe of the apartment across from hers. She looked like she belonged here, like she belonged everywhere. A messy bun of dark, wild curls sat atop her head. She wore a battered leather jacket slung over a simple black tank top, tight jeans, and scuffed boots that looked like they had survived more than one street fight. There was something magnetic about her — something fiercely alive but guarded — like a stray cat who would let you feed it but never let you get too close. Her eyes, deep green and watchful, flicked over Savannah quickly — assessing, reading.

Savannah shifted the bags awkwardly. "I'm good," she said, fumbling for her keys.

The girl smirked and pushed off the doorframe, sauntering over to pluck two bags neatly from Savannah's overloaded arms. "You looked like you were about to lose the whole operation," she said, tossing the bags onto

Savannah's kitchen counter with a theatrical sigh. "No shame. These city steps are brutal."

Savannah laughed despite herself. "You're not wrong."

The girl stuck out her hand, her grip firm and grounding. "Valarie Townsend," she said. "But friends call me Val."

"Savannah Lacroix," Savannah replied, smiling warmly.

"New neighbor, huh?" Val said, leaning back against the counter like she owned the place.

"Yeah. Just moved in yesterday," Savannah said. "Starting at NYU next week."

Val's eyes flickered — a quick flash of something darker — but the grin returned almost instantly, sharp and easy. "Smart girl," she said. "NYU's no joke."

They moved around the tiny kitchen, unpacking groceries like old roommates falling into rhythm. Outside the cracked window, a siren wailed, the sound bouncing off brick walls and steel scaffolding. Someone was arguing on the sidewalk below — angry words cut short by the sudden bark of laughter. The city was alive and breathing around them, relentless and vibrant.

Savannah tucked a loaf of bread into the pantry and stole a glance at Val, who was examining a can of coffee like it held secrets. "You from New York?" Savannah asked.

Val shrugged, tossing the can onto the counter with a clatter. "Born here," she said. "Bounced around a lot. Mostly Manhattan, but... you know how it is." Her voice trailed off briefly, an edge slipping through the casual words — something heavy she didn't want to explain.

Savannah hesitated but let it pass. She knew what it was to carry stories too heavy to hand to strangers. "Must be nice," Savannah said lightly. "Knowing where you're going. Knowing where you belong."

Val's smile twisted slightly, bittersweet. "Yeah," she said. "You could say that."

As they worked, Val pointed out her favorite places with the easy confidence of someone who had lived a thousand lives in these streets.

"You'll want to avoid the Q train after midnight," she said, tossing Savannah a stick of gum. "Trust me. And there's a pizza place two blocks over that'll change your life, but only after midnight. During the day, it's a crime scene."

Savannah laughed, popping the gum into her mouth. "Sounds like insider knowledge."

Val grinned. "Stick with me, country girl. I'll teach you how to survive."

Savannah arched a brow. "Country girl?"

Val grinned, pointing at Savannah's jeans and giving a playful tilt of her head. 'Between those and that Southern lilt, "Dead giveaway," she teased. "But don't worry. New York loves a good accent."

Savannah chuckled, feeling herself relax.

There was something about Val — a rough-edged kindness — that felt genuine, even if Savannah could sense there were cracks beneath the surface. A tiny voice in her mind — her grandmother's voice — whispered caution.

But Savannah pushed it aside.

They finished unpacking, and Val perched on the counter, swinging her boots against the cabinet door. "You'll get the hang of it," Val said, flashing a crooked smile. "New York's like a bad boyfriend. It'll beat you up sometimes, make you swear you'll never come back... but then you do, 'cause damn, those good days? They make you feel invincible."

Savannah laughed, shaking her head. "That's... comforting, in a weird way."

Val winked. "Hey, I survive, don't I?"

Savannah nodded, feeling a warmth unfurl in her chest. Maybe — just maybe — making friends here wouldn't be as impossible as she had feared.

Later, after Val had finally sauntered back to her own apartment with a casual, "See you around, neighbor," Savannah lingered in the doorway. The apartment felt different now. Lighter. Less empty.

She leaned her head against the doorframe and

closed her eyes, letting the sounds of the city drift around her. The rattle of subway trains beneath the streets. The hum of traffic. The soft, distant strains of someone playing jazz on a battered old saxophone.

She smiled. It had been a long time since laughter — real laughter — had echoed through her life. Maybe New York would be harder than she imagined. Maybe it would bruise her, break her in unexpected ways. But maybe...it would heal her too.

Somewhere deep inside, buried beneath excitement and fear, Savannah's grandmother's voice stirred. "Not every smiling face is a friend, chère. Trust your spirit — not just your eyes."

Savannah shivered slightly but pushed the thought away. For now, she had a neighbor. A friend. And in a city as big and wild as New York, that felt like a small miracle.

Chapter 4: Roots of the Past

Savannah tightened the strap of her bag over her shoulder and navigated the crowded sidewalks leading to NYU's campus. The day was crisp and blustery, the autumn air sharp enough to bite at her cheeks. Ahead, Washington Square Park sprawled out like an open stage, the famous marble arch rising proudly against a cloud-mottled sky.

Street musicians gathered in small groups — a saxophonist weaving lazy notes into the breeze, a guitarist singing low and rough about lost love. Vendors hawked roasted chestnuts and warm pretzels, their carts sending up tempting spirals of buttery steam. Students hurried past her in every direction, laughing, arguing, sipping coffee, shouting across the crowded square. The ground was littered with fallen leaves in fiery reds and golds, swirling around the feet of skateboarders carving lazy circles through the crowds. The city didn't just move — it hummed.

Savannah paused for a moment at the edge of the park, clutching her bag strap tighter. This was why she had come. To be part of something bigger, older, deeper.

Her mind drifted briefly back to her grandmother's porch — the warm nights, the slow dance of fireflies across the bayou — and the stories whispered over rocking chairs. "Cities carry spirits too, chère," her grandmother had said once. "Not ghosts. Memory. And not every memory is kind." A shiver chased down Savannah's spine, but she shook it off.

Today was about beginnings. Drawing a deep breath, she pushed forward into the thrumming heart of the university.

Finding the lecture hall was a minor adventure in itself. The history department was tucked into an old building with cracked marble floors and hallways that twisted like a labyrinth. The walls were lined with heavy velvet curtains and tarnished bronze plaques, memorializing forgotten scholars and benefactors.

Savannah wandered past shadowed alcoves and tall, arched windows, feeling small and new and thrillingly insignificant. Her boots clicked against the worn floors, the sound swallowed quickly by the massive, echoing halls.

Finally, she spotted Room 304. The heavy oak door was slightly ajar, and murmured voices drifted out — students chatting, the rustle of papers. Savannah slipped inside quietly.

The lecture hall was tiered, steep rows of old wood benches curving toward a low platform where a chalkboard and old pull-down projector screen dominated the wall. She chose a seat near the middle — not too close, not too hidden — and pulled out her battered leather notebook and a pen.

The door at the front creaked open. And in strode Dr. Adrian Monroe. He wasn't what Savannah expected. Instead of a stooped academic weighed down by tweed and dusty books, Monroe moved with the sharp grace of a predator. Lean and wiry, with silver-streaked hair pulled back into a low knot, he surveyed the room with piercing gray eyes that seemed to weigh and measure each student before dismissing them. His clothes were simple — black slacks, a charcoal sweater, and worn leather shoes — but somehow, they seemed more formal than a suit. He carried authority the way a sword carried an edge — not visible until it cut you.

"Welcome," he said, voice low and clipped. "This course will not be easy. It will require your mind — and possibly your soul — if you do it right."

A few students chuckled awkwardly.

Savannah didn't. There was something behind his words — a kind of stillness, an unspoken truth — that made her sit up straighter.

The first lecture was intoxicating.

Dr. Monroe spoke not only of ancient civilizations but of the unseen threads binding past and present. Slides flickered across the screen behind him: Crumbling temples devoured by jungle. Charms carved from bone and ivory. Stone medallions etched with spiraling symbols that seemed to move if you looked too long.

One slide made Savannah's breath catch.

A medallion — no larger than a silver dollar — carved from black stone, the spiral pattern so intricate it seemed almost alive. Under the dim lights, it gleamed with an oily, unnatural sheen. Binding Charm. Origin Unknown, read the caption beneath.

Savannah leaned forward in her seat, her heart thudding. There was something about it — a pull, a hum she couldn't explain. It felt familiar. Like a memory just out of reach.

After class, the other students poured out in noisy, chattering clumps, oblivious to the storm Monroe had stirred. Savannah wandered into the university's library, still dazed. The library was an ancient, towering place — floor after floor of dusty shelves and towering windows that filtered in the cold gray light. She wandered the rows aimlessly, trailing her fingers along cracked leather spines, the smell of old paper and forgotten secrets wrapping around her. She pulled down books on relics, ancient societies, ritual practices — piling them into her arms until she could barely see over the top.

"It's just research," she told herself. "Curiosity. Nothing more." But a deeper voice inside whispered otherwise. Maybe she wasn't just chasing knowledge. Maybe she was chasing something that had always been chasing her.

By the time Savannah left campus, the sky had darkened into a deep, velvet indigo. Streetlamps flickered to life, and students spilled out of the university buildings, laughing, arguing, wrapped in scarves and heavy coats. Savannah tucked her hands deep into her jacket pockets and started toward the subway station.

That's when she felt it. At first, it was just a prickling along the back of her neck — a static hum in the air. She quickened her steps instinctively, glancing over her shoulder. Nothing. Just strangers. Busy, distracted, harmless. Probably just nerves.

She ducked her head and moved faster, weaving through the crowd. Halfway down the grimy steps to the subway, she glanced back again. And caught it. A figure — dark, motionless — lingering just at the mouth of a shadowed alley. Watching. Her heart slammed into her ribs. The figure stepped back, swallowed by the shadows. Gone.

Savannah forced herself forward, each step heavier than the last. She shoved through the turnstiles and onto the crowded subway platform, pressing herself into a corner near a steel pillar. The crowd buzzed around her, students and workers and tourists blending into a blur.

But Savannah stayed rigid, her eyes sweeping every face. Every hand. Every shadow.

The train roared into the station and she boarded quickly, wedging herself into a corner seat where she could see everyone. She kept her bag clutched to her chest, fingers trembling slightly. She told herself it was nothing. Just nerves. Just city life. Just Dr. Monroe's ghost stories getting under her skin.

But deep inside — deeper than reason — Savannah

knew better. The city had welcomed her. The city had claimed her. And something had started to see her. Really see her.

Chapter 5: The Invitation

The days slipped into rhythm like notes in a jazz melody.

Each morning, Savannah tightened the strap of her bag, slung her crossbody purse over one shoulder, and set out along the tree-lined streets toward NYU. She walked beneath the canopy of yellowing leaves, her earbuds feeding her soft jazz or old French ballads, the city's noise fading into a comfortable hum.

The smells of the city changed as the weather cooled: roasted chestnuts from corner vendors, the thick aroma of brewing coffee from sidewalk cafés, the dusty scent of books and pavement when it rained.

Every day, she wove herself a little deeper into the

city's living fabric — a familiar nod from the barista at Hollow & Bean, a favorite spot in Washington Square Park where the morning sun hit just right, the small thrill of recognizing subway lines without needing to check her phone.

Her classes at NYU were demanding, exhilarating, a strange kind of joy. Ancient languages filled her notebooks: sweeping characters, strange markings. She spent long hours at the library, buried among tomes thick with dust, chasing the threads of civilizations so old they had no names left to claim them.

New York was still vast and overwhelming sometimes — a living organism that could chew you up if you stumbled — but it was also becoming... hers. Piece by piece.

And nearly every day, she stopped at Hollow & Bean. The café had become her anchor — her quiet between movements. She always ordered the same thing now: the lavender latte Jamie had once suggested. At first, it had been a small tribute. A memory she could smile about. But as the days stretched into weeks, Savannah realized it had become something else. A habit threaded with hope.

Every time the bell above the café door chimed, she looked up - heart lifting - and every time, it wasn't him. A mother dragging a stroller. A student on his phone. A woman in a business suit. Never Jamie.

She scolded herself for being ridiculous, for clinging to a stranger like a shipwrecked sailor to driftwood. But still, she looked up. Still, she hoped. Sometimes she wondered if he even remembered her at all. Still, she ordered the lavender latte. Still, she saved him a place in the story she was weaving.

If Hollow & Bean was Savannah's anchor, Val was her whirlwind. Wild, messy, brilliant Val - who could cross a street against oncoming traffic with a grin and a middle finger raised high. Val who knew every cracked alleyway shortcut and every secret late-night diner. Val who seemed too young and too old at the same time as if she had lived twice as much life crammed into half as many years.

They explored the city like conquerors: A grimy record store where Savannah found a scratched Billie Holiday vinyl. A bookstore that smelled like mildew and magic, with ladders that slid along towering shelves. An open mic night so terrible Savannah had to stifle her laughter in a greasy slice of pizza. They rode the subway with no particular destination, just to watch the city unfold — to see businessmen nodding off, women in glittering saris, breakdancers spinning miracles on the platform.

One rainy afternoon, they got caught in a sudden downpour, shrieking and laughing as they sprinted back to Wren House, soaked to the bone.

Val taught Savannah how to jaywalk without hesitation - "Walk like you own the street, girl." She even taught her the art of pretending you belonged somewhere you didn't — an important skill in New York.

"If you act like you're meant to be there," Val said with a smirk, "half the battle's won."

Savannah teased her about her 'life hacks' but secretly treasured every lesson.

New York was still a wild ocean, but Val was a rough, brilliant buoy she could cling to. They shared greasy takeout on the front steps some nights, sipping cheap wine from paper cups, laughing at nothing and everything.

But there were small cracks too. Tiny moments where the easy laughter faltered.

Once, wandering through a vintage bookstore tucked away in the East Village, Savannah found an old anthropology textbook. She flipped it open to a page describing ancient relics used by secret societies — charms and totems meant to bind members to their cause.

"Fascinating," Savannah mused aloud, tracing the illustration of a spiraling amulet. "Imagine believing an object could control you. Terrifying."

Val's laugh came too quickly. Tight. Almost forced. "People still believe that crap?" she said, eyes fixed not on the book but on the window beyond.

Savannah frowned slightly, sensing the moment shift, but said nothing. The moment passed. Like a ripple over still water. But somewhere deep in her gut, a whisper stirred.

It was late Friday afternoon when the invitation came.

Savannah stumbled into her apartment after back-to-back classes and a long library shift, arms laden with textbooks and a half-eaten muffin.

Val was already sprawled on her couch, legs dangling off the side, flipping through channels like she owned the place.

Savannah raised an eyebrow. "Jesus, do you live here now?"

Val smirked, tossing the remote onto the coffee table. "It's called being neighborly. You're welcome."

Savannah dropped her bags and collapsed into the armchair opposite her.

"Got plans tomorrow night?" Val asked casually, twirling a curl around her finger.

Savannah narrowed her eyes suspiciously. "Define 'plans.'"

"There's this gathering," Val said. "Not a party-party. More like... a salon. Cool people. Writers, artists, a few older women who've been around the block a few times."

Savannah blinked. "Older women?"

Val laughed. "Trust me, they're cooler than we are. Think scarves and red wine and quoting Oscar Wilde at 2 a.m."

Savannah smiled despite herself. "Sounds... bohemian."

"It's chill," Val promised. "Wine. Books. Music. No weird cult stuff. Probably."

Savannah hesitated. A voice inside her — old and soft like a remembered hymn — whispered caution. "Not every open hand is a hand you should take, chère."

But Val was looking at her with those wild, mischievous green eyes. And Savannah... trusted her. "Okay," she said, tossing her hands up in surrender. "But if they try to sacrifice me to a relic, I'm out."

Val whooped and texted furiously, already making plans.

Savannah laughed, feeling the last of her doubts scatter like leaves in the wind.

That night, after Savannah had curled up in bed with a battered novel, Val lay awake in her own apartment, staring at the cracked ceiling. The past rose around her in slow, poisonous waves. A blanket on a subway grate. A mother with trembling hands, whispering stories that dissolved with the dawn. Nights spent hungry, cold, forgotten. She remembered learning to lie before she learned to tie her shoes.

She remembered how Vivian found her — how easily she'd traded her soul for safety without even knowing the cost.

And now... Savannah. Bright. Trusting. Whole. Val didn't want to hurt her. She didn't want to drag her into the darkness. But the threads were already tangled. And the hands pulling them were stronger than love or loyalty or guilt.

"I'm sorry," Val thought, staring into the dark. "I'm so sorry."

But she would do what she was told. Because survival, in the end, was the only song Val had ever learned how to sing.

Chapter 6: The Gathering

The sun was beginning its slow descent behind the trees as the car turned off the main highway and onto a long, winding road bordered by towering oaks. Savannah pressed her forehead lightly against the cool glass window, feeling the shift in the world around her. The hum of the city faded behind them, replaced by the hush of leaves and the golden hush of twilight.

She watched as the concrete and glass gave way to shadowed woods. The air grew heavier, older, scented faintly with damp earth and something sweet — honeysuckle, maybe.

"It's like something out of a novel," she murmured.

Val, seated beside her, grinned and blew a bubble

with her gum. "Told you it was fancy. Old money fancy. Like Gatsby-level stuff."

They curved through dense woods, headlights flashing against gnarled trunks and draping moss. Savannah felt it in her bones — they weren't just leaving the city. They were crossing into another world. A world untouched by sirens and skyscrapers. A world that had been waiting long before she was born.

The trees parted at last to reveal a set of tall, wrought-iron gates, their black curves twisting like vines around twin stone pillars. A crest was etched into the stone — so worn by time it was almost illegible — but something about it prickled at Savannah's memory. The car slowed. The gates creaked open on ancient hinges with a sound like a sigh, and they drove forward into a different kind of silence — heavy, expectant, alive.

The Sinclair estate rose before them like something carved from a dream — or perhaps a nightmare, depending on the eye. A sprawling mansion of weathered gray stone, ivy clawing up its sides, chimneys reaching toward the bruised sky. The windows glowed with warm golden light, casting halos over manicured gardens and stone statues half-sunk into the ground like forgotten gods. Marble nymphs peeked through trimmed hedges. The driveway curved in a wide, graceful arc toward a grand staircase framed by heavy iron lanterns already flickering against the dusk.

Savannah pressed a hand lightly against her chest. "Wow," she whispered.

Val gave her a wink. "Wait till you see inside."

There was something playful in her voice — but something tight underneath it too. Savannah tucked the feeling away.

Inside, the mansion was elegance raised to the level of myth. Polished wood floors stretched in endless gleaming rivers. Chandeliers the size of small cars dripped light like diamonds from the soaring ceilings. Fireplaces crackled softly in cavernous rooms, their warmth battling the lingering coolness of the old stone. The air smelled of firewood, old paper, lavender, and — faintly — something metallic.

Guests in graceful clothing mingled in small groups, their laughter soft, their voices measured, their glances sharp. It was a performance, Savannah realized. Every gesture, every compliment, every sparkling laugh was rehearsed — smooth as worn glass.

Val pressed a glass of wine into her hand, steering her through the current of faces with practiced ease.

Savannah sipped and smiled and answered polite questions about her studies, her background, her dreams.

"You have such poise," a woman in pearls cooed.

"You must come again," a thin man with a silver pocket watch insisted.

It was flattering. It was intoxicating. It was — Savannah thought uneasily — just a little too perfect.

A ripple passed through the crowd like the hush before a storm. Two women entered the grand hall, and the very air seemed to part around them. Vivian Sinclair, radiant in emerald silk, her silver-blonde hair swept into a chignon so elegant it seemed sculpted from marble. Victoria Sinclair followed beside her — a quieter, more commanding presence. Where Vivian dazzled, Victoria loomed.

Vivian's sharp eyes swept the room — seeking, measuring — and then landed on Savannah. Her smile widened, gracious and disarming. "Ah," she said, her voice like velvet and wine. "You must be Savannah Lacroix."

Vivian moved forward and took Savannah's hands between hers — warm, firm, deliberate. "We've heard such delightful things about you. You shine, my dear. It's impossible not to notice."

Savannah blushed, unused to such direct adoration.

Victoria stepped forward silently. Her gray eyes — sharp, ancient — studied Savannah's face with surgical precision. "You have your grandmother's eyes," she said softly.

Savannah froze. She hadn't mentioned her grandmother to anyone. A tiny chill crept up her spine.

Vivian laughed lightly, brushing the tension aside.

"Victoria notices things most of us don't, dear. She's gifted that way. Don't let it spook you."

Savannah managed a small smile, but her mind whirled.

Vivian linked her arm casually through Savannah's and steered her away from the crowd. "Walk with me, darling," she said.

They moved into a smaller side room — a sunroom full of tall windows, velvet armchairs, and the warm, faded scent of old roses. The music and laughter from the hall faded into a distant hum.

Vivian sat gracefully on a tufted bench and gestured for Savannah to join her. "I like to know who's in my home," she said gently.

Savannah sat, perching on the edge of the seat.

"You have the air of someone who doesn't quite realize her worth," Vivian continued, her voice low and hypnotic.

Savannah ducked her head, smiling awkwardly. "I'm

just a grad student. Ancient civilizations and dead languages."

Vivian's eyes gleamed. "And you've come a long way to chase that dream."

Savannah hesitated, then — drawn by the warmth in Vivian's voice — spoke the truth. "I lost my parents when I was in high school," she said softly. "After that, I moved in with my grandmother down in the Louisiana bayou. She raised me."

Vivian's hand tightened briefly around hers. "It sounds like she gave you the kind of strength that can't be taught," she said.

Savannah nodded, a small ache blooming in her chest. "She did."

"And she's still there?"

"Yes."

Vivian's smile softened even further. "You're carrying more with you than you realize, dear one."

As they stood to rejoin the party, Savannah lingered

for a second near a walnut cabinet lined with antique relics. One piece — a small stone medallion under glass — caught her eye. It was carved with tight spirals, ancient and deliberate. Her breath caught. It was almost identical to the Binding Charm Dr. Monroe had shown in class. Her fingers itched to reach for it, to trace the grooves.

Vivian noticed and smiled too brightly. "Oh, that old thing?" she said airily. "Just a family keepsake. Nothing special."

But Savannah saw it. The flicker. The shadow behind her eyes.

The crowd shifted again.

Vivian clapped her hands lightly, drawing everyone's attention. "My sons have arrived."

The double doors opened wide. Jamie Sinclair walked in first — and Savannah's heart stuttered.

He looked just as she remembered — dark hair curling slightly, gray eyes warm and crinkling at the corners when he smiled.

Beside him came Jasper Sinclair — his twin but different. Sharper. Harder. Where Jamie's warmth invited, Jasper's gaze pinned.

Savannah's stomach tightened instinctively.

Vivian ushered them closer. "Jamie, Jasper — meet Savannah."

Jasper stepped forward first, all polished charm and dangerous grace. He took Savannah's hand, his touch cool and lingering. "Pleasure to meet you," he said smoothly. Savannah caught it — the tattoo. A small black number "2," nestled between his thumb and forefinger. Her skin prickled. She smiled politely, withdrawing her hand as quickly as manners allowed.

Her gaze drifted back to Jamie — and relief flooded her chest. Jamie smiled — softer, more genuine. "Hey," he said.

Savannah laughed lightly. "Hi." It was silly. It was everything.

They found a quiet alcove near the garden windows.

Jamie leaned casually against the frame, looking suddenly — achingly — boyish.

"I was hoping I'd run into you again after the café," he said. "But... I didn't think it'd be like this."

Savannah smiled, heart hammering. "It's been almost a year."

"Way too long," he said. "Maybe we shouldn't leave it to chance anymore."

He pulled out his phone, offering it shyly. "Can I get your number?" Their fingers brushed as she took it, and the touch was electric. As she handed it back, her eyes wandered across the crowd again. And froze.

Professor Adrian Monroe. He stood deep in conversation with Victoria Sinclair, his face unusually grave. Savannah stiffened. Jamie followed her gaze. "The Sinclairs fund a lot of NYU programs," he said. "Monroe's basically part of the family."

Savannah nodded — but the knowledge left a sour taste in her mouth. Monroe didn't look at her. Didn't acknowledge her. It was as if he had wiped her from existence.

The evening wound down. Val appeared at her side, bright and laughing. "Come on, city girl. Time to go."

But Jamie stepped forward. "I'll walk you to the car."

The night air was cool and clean, stars struggling against the distant lights of the city. At the car, Jamie lingered. "Text me when you get home?" he said. Savannah nodded, feeling suddenly shy. "I will."

He smiled — that real, heart-stealing smile — and opened the door for her.

As they pulled away, Savannah glanced back. Jasper and Victoria stood in the grand doorway, framed by the light, their faces shadowed and unreadable. Watching. Waiting. The chill returned.

She pulled her jacket tighter around herself, willing the unease away. It was just the wine. Just the grandeur. Just nerves. At least, that's what she told herself. For now.

Chapter 7: The Forgotten Journal

The hum of voices filled the NYU student lounge, a background blur against Savannah's swirling thoughts. She sat curled into a deep armchair near the tall windows, notebook closed on her lap, eyes unfocused as they traced the slow drift of clouds across the courtyard outside. The scent of strong coffee, ink, and rain-damp wool filled the air, mingling with the faint strains of a jazz trio playing softly from someone's speaker. Class would start in twenty minutes. Plenty of time to think. Too much time, maybe.

She couldn't stop replaying the night before. The grandeur of the Sinclair estate — its sprawling gardens, its suffocating beauty. The glittering, too-perfect guests who spoke in polished tones and offered smiles sharp enough to cut. The icy elegance of Vivian and Victoria, moving through the crowd like queens among pawns. The Binding Charm she had glimpsed behind glass — so familiar, so wrong.

And Jamie — warm, kind, real. The only thing about that evening that had felt genuine. Her fingers tightened around the edges of her notebook. Jamie. She smiled a little at the thought of him — remembering the quiet warmth in his voice, the way his hand had brushed against hers. But the smile faded almost as quickly. No text. No call. Nothing. Maybe he was busy. Maybe he didn't feel the pull she felt. Maybe it was all in her head.

And then there was Val. Val, who had swept her so easily into that strange, glittering world. How did she even know people like the Sinclairs? Savannah had never asked. It hadn't seemed important. Now, the thought gnawed at her like a loose thread.

Her grandmother's voice echoed faintly across the years — "Truth often wears a pretty face, chère. Trust your spirit, not just your eyes."

Savannah shivered, brushing the thought away.

The heavy doors of the lecture hall loomed just ahead. Savannah stood, gathering her things, heart fluttering unevenly. Ancient Relics and Cultures awaited. And somehow... she had the terrible feeling she was walking into something she didn't yet understand.

The lecture hall buzzed lightly with conversation as students trickled in, their voices bouncing off the vaulted ceiling. Savannah slipped into her usual seat near the middle, trying to steady her nerves as she flipped open her notebook.

Professor Monroe entered a moment later, carrying his worn leather satchel and a stack of yellowed notes. He looked the same — gray hair slicked neatly back, black sweater sharp against the pale glow of the projector screen — but something about him felt different today. Sharper. Tighter. Darker.

He wasted no time. Today's lecture was not about cities or artifacts or trade routes. It was about power. Real power. He spoke of secret orders — families who had passed down relics not for wealth, but for dominion. Not to preserve history, but to control it.

"Some societies," Monroe said, voice low and cutting, "believed that true loyalty could not be earned. It had to be taken."

A hush settled over the room. Slides flashed overhead: Rings carved with ancient symbols. Broken amulets blackened by fire. Bone necklaces strung together in intricate, binding patterns.

Savannah scribbled furiously, her hand trembling slightly.

Monroe's eyes swept the room — not lingering anywhere — until they landed on her. Just for a moment. Savannah stiffened. The look was not hostile. Not cruel. It was worse. It was knowing. A silent question she didn't yet understand. Her stomach twisted, but she didn't look away.

After class, she hesitated by the door, notebook clutched tightly against her chest. Most students filed out quickly, eager for freedom and coffee.

When Monroe finally packed his materials, Savannah stepped forward. "Professor Monroe?" she said, heart hammering.

He glanced up, his face unreadable.

"I think I saw you last night," Savannah said, forcing a casual tone. "At... a gathering."

Monroe's mouth twitched — not a smile, not a sneer. "I saw you as well, Miss Lacroix." He adjusted the strap of his satchel, his movements crisp, almost mechanical. "I have longstanding ties to the Sinclair family. University patronage, historical collaborations." His voice was clipped, precise — as if reading from a script. "But I do not... fraternize with students outside the classroom."

Savannah flushed. "Oh — of course. I didn't mean _ "

He waved her off with a flick of his hand. "You show genuine curiosity," he said, his tone softening slightly. "It's rare."

Savannah blinked, unsure how to respond.

"If you are serious about your studies," Monroe continued, "I lead a private Advanced Studies Group. Invitation only."

Savannah's heart leapt. "I'd love to," she said.

He nodded briskly. "Wednesdays. Six o'clock. Room 512 — North Hall." He turned away before she could ask anything more, falling into quiet conversation with another student.

Savannah lingered a moment longer, the invitation burning a hole in her chest. Pride. Excitement. And an unease she couldn't quite name.

That evening, Savannah sat curled cross-legged on her bed, laptop forgotten beside her, the soft buzz of traffic leaking through the cracked window.

She checked her phone again. Nothing. The screen glowed with stubborn silence. She tossed it aside with a groan, flopping back against the pillows. Maybe she had imagined it all. Maybe Jamie was just being polite. Maybe he had someone else. The ache was sharper than she expected. Why did she care so much? Maybe because — for one wild moment — she had believed she wasn't alone in the world anymore.

Her gaze drifted to the stack of boxes still piled in the corner of her room. And she remembered. The journal. Her heart kicked against her ribs. Sliding off the bed, Savannah knelt beside the boxes, digging through old photo albums, scarves, paperbacks. Her fingers found it at last — wrapped carefully in a linen cloth, just as her grandmother had left it.

She pulled it free, hands trembling slightly. The leather cover was worn smooth with years of touch, the faint scent of gardenias clinging to it still. For a long moment, Savannah simply held it against her chest, breathing deeply. Her grandmother's voice seemed to whisper through the dusty pages: "Find your roots, chère. Even when they're buried deep."

She pulled back the cloth and opened the journal carefully, the spine creaking like a door half-forgotten. The pages were filled with delicate, looping script — French and English blending together in a soft, rhythmic dance. She skimmed the first few entries — recipes, herbal remedies, scraps of prayers — feeling a pang of homesickness so fierce it almost doubled her over.

"*Protection is in the knowing,*" one page read. "*A covenant can be broken — but only with blood, love, and the name unspoken.*" Savannah frowned, tracing the words with her fingertip. They sent a shiver down her spine. She leaned closer, eager to read more.

A sharp knock shattered the quiet. Savannah jumped, heart hammering, clutching the journal to her chest. She crossed the small apartment and cracked the door. Val stood there, grinning, a bottle of cheap champagne swinging from her hand.

"Girl!" she said brightly. "Get dressed — we're going out!"

Savannah laughed, breathless. "Now?"

"Yes, now!" Val insisted, pushing inside like a whirlwind. "Some of my other friends are dying to meet you. You can't say no."

Savannah glanced back at the bed — the open journal, the words still whispering.

"I was kind of in the middle of—"

Val pouted dramatically. "Please? You've been locked up in here like a nun."

Savannah hesitated. The journal seemed to pulse in the corner of her vision. A door half-opened. A choice laid bare. But Val's hand was warm around hers, pulling, pleading. Savannah laughed, letting herself be tugged toward the closet.

"Okay," she said. "But I'm not wearing heels."

"Deal," Val said, tossing a hoodie at her. "Tonight, you're officially one of us."

As Savannah pulled on jeans and boots, she caught one last glance at the journal lying open on the bed. The soft linen cloth had slipped halfway off, exposing the faded leather and the pages scrawled in a hand she could almost hear humming. "*A covenant can be broken...*" The words echoed in her mind like a bell tolling in thick fog. Savannah shook her head. One night wouldn't change anything. The journal would still be there tomorrow. Waiting. Watching. Waiting.

Chapter 8: The Inner Circle

Val was relentless.

"You're not wearing that," she declared, elbow-deep in Savannah's closet, casting judgment like a seasoned queen.

Savannah perched on the edge of her bed, watching helplessly as sweaters, jeans, and simple dresses flew through the air.

"It's cute," Val said, flinging a soft cardigan onto the floor. "But tonight? You need something... electric."

Savannah laughed, tossing a pillow at her. "It's just

a get-together, right?"

Val grinned wickedly. "The right outfit turns a get-together into a night you don't forget."

Finally, with a triumphant whoop, Val yanked free a sleek black dress Savannah barely remembered owning — all smooth lines and whispered promises.

She flung it onto the bed.

"This," Val said. "Trust me."

Half an hour later, Savannah stood in front of her mirror, adjusting the hem of the dress. It clung in all the right places, the neckline dipping just daringly enough. Her hair was loose and tumbling down her back, makeup precise but dramatic — dark eyeliner, a splash of lipstick, Val's touch quick and deft.

"You look incredible," Val said, hands on her hips, surveying her handiwork like a proud artist.

Savannah smiled — but a flicker of unease twisted in her stomach. Behind her on the bed, half-buried in pillows, lay the journal. Waiting. Calling. Not tonight.

Savannah shoved the thought away, grabbing her jacket. Tonight was for fun.

The lounge was tucked away down a narrow side street Savannah would have missed without Val leading the way. Dim golden lights glowed above the heavy wooden door, and a black-clad doorman nodded curtly as Val leaned in and whispered something Savannah couldn't quite hear. Inside, the lounge was a hidden jewel — walls draped in deep velvet, smoky glass lamps casting soft amber halos, polished floors gleaming underfoot. The air smelled of spiced wine, old wood, and the faint, heady musk of sandalwood incense. Low music pulsed from hidden speakers — jazzy, sultry, hypnotic. It was like stepping into another world — lush, intimate, untouchable. Savannah hesitated just inside the door, overwhelmed.

Val threw an arm around her shoulders. "Welcome to the real New York," she whispered.

They weaved through the crowd — elegant, murmuring clusters of people sipping from crystal glasses. Everywhere they went, Val was greeted with smiles, cheek kisses, murmured jokes. It seemed like everyone knew her. At a cozy corner booth, a small group waved them over.

"Savi, meet the crew!" Val beamed.

Names blurred together:

• Cara — tall, angular, with a smoker's laugh and kohl-smudged eyes.

• Luca — wiry, restless, flicking a silver coin between his fingers.

• Simone — silver hair cascading down her back, a voice like velvet.

• Oliver — soft-spoken, smiling with a kind of secret sadness.

They welcomed Savannah like an old friend.

"You have the kindest eyes," Simone said, studying her with a tilt of her head.

"Old soul," Luca added, flipping the coin and catching it expertly.

"Destined," Cara murmured, raising her glass.

Savannah laughed, embarrassed but warmed. A glass of champagne found its way into her hand, and she sipped it — feeling the tight coil of the day begin to loosen.

Conversation turned strange but fascinating. Destiny. Legacies. The invisible threads that tied people to fate.

Simone leaned close, her perfume thick and dizzying. "You," she whispered, "have an ancient spirit. I can feel it." Savannah blushed, brushing it off with a laugh. But deep inside, something shivered awake.

Later, needing air, Savannah slipped away to the balcony. The city sprawled before her, loud and brilliant — a chaos of neon, traffic, life. She leaned against the cold iron railing, letting the wind whip her hair into her face. Her hand hovered over her phone. Text him? Would she seem desperate? Pathetic? She pressed her lips together, battling herself. Finally, with a breathless rush, she typed: *Hey, hope your day went well.* Sent.

The message hovered there, unread. Savannah tucked the phone away and stared at the lights. Maybe he wouldn't reply. Maybe it didn't matter.

Behind her, the door creaked. Val appeared, smiling like the cat who owned the world. "Don't disappear," she teased, linking her arm through Savannah's. "They love you in there."

Savannah smiled — a little tighter now — and allowed herself to be pulled back inside.

The night blurred into more laughter, more drinks. But underneath the easy smiles and clinking glasses, there was a thread. A pulse. A rhythm. Mentions of tradition. Of family lines. Of unseen forces.

At one point, Cara raised her glass in a solemn toast. "To rebirth through reflection," she said. The others echoed it — voices low and reverent. Savannah clinked glasses with them, swept up in the moment.

Later, Simone — silver-haired and sharp-eyed — leaned across the table. "We should have you make a pledge," she teased, a twinkle in her eye.

"Just a small one," Oliver added, voice mild.

Savannah laughed uneasily. "Pledge what?"

"That you'll always find your true path," Simone said smoothly.

"A small vow," Cara added, swirling her wine. "Nothing binding."

The others watched her — smiling, relaxed. Waiting. Savannah's chest tightened.

Her grandmother's voice — "Never promise what your soul doesn't understand, chère."

She smiled, light and airy, and raised her glass instead. "I think I'll pledge to survive my first semester without flunking."

The others laughed, the moment passing. But the tightness didn't leave her chest.

Near midnight, Savannah found herself slumped into the velvet cushions, laughing at a ridiculous story Luca was telling, when Val's phone buzzed sharply. Val glanced down — and her face shifted. For the briefest second, the mask slipped. Fear. Real, raw fear. But it was gone just as fast, replaced by her usual bright grin.

"Uh, shoot," she said, swinging to her feet. "Vivian needs me."

Savannah blinked. "Now?"

Val shrugged, slipping on her jacket. "Family," she said simply. "You don't say no." She leaned in, pressing a quick kiss to Savannah's cheek. "I called a car for you. It'll be waiting."

Savannah wanted to protest — to ask what was wrong — but Val was already moving, weaving through the crowd. Through the glass doors, Savannah caught a glimpse of her — slipping into the night with a young man she didn't recognize, their heads bent close. Gone.

The ride home was a quiet hum, the driver silent, the city a blur of lights and shadows. Savannah leaned her head against the cold glass, exhaustion washing over her. She thought of Val — Vivian — the Sinclair estate — the strange words and stranger smiles. Something gnawed at her chest, sharp and restless.

Back at her apartment, she peeled off her dress, tossing it over the chair, and padded barefoot to the bed. The journal waited there. Silent. Patient. She ran her fingers lightly over the cracked leather. "Tomorrow," she whispered. "Tomorrow."

Sliding under the covers, she checked her phone one last time. A new message blinked on the screen. Jamie. *Sorry for the late reply. Crazy day. Thought about you. Hope we can see each other soon.* Simple. Guarded. But warm. Savannah smiled — small, real, aching. Maybe New York wasn't so cold after all.

Chapter 9: A Wish in the Dark

Savannah stood in front of her closet, biting her lip, the soft buzz of her phone pulling her from her spiraling thoughts. She already knew who it was — and what it was about.

Her heart hammered as she snatched the phone from her bedspread.

The message was simple, sweet, almost formal in its careful phrasing: *Would you have dinner with me at the estate tonight? 7:30? Jamie.*

Her fingers hovered over the screen for a second longer than necessary before she typed back: I'd love to. Three words that didn't even begin to capture the wild rush of hope blooming inside her chest. She set the phone down and turned to the mirror, studying her reflection critically.

What does one wear when stepping into a fairy tale?

After rifling through nearly everything she owned, Savannah chose a dress softer than what she usually wore — a silky navy that reminded her of the midnight sky after a southern summer storm. She let her hair fall naturally around her shoulders, loose waves framing her face, her mother's gold cross resting at her collarbone like a secret talisman. Simple. Beautiful. Hopeful.

Before leaving, she glanced once toward the corner of her room, where the worn leather journal rested on her nightstand. Waiting. Always waiting. "Later," she promised silently, smoothing the fabric of her dress. Tonight wasn't for questions. It was for dreams.

The Sinclair mansion looked different at night. It breathed. The heavy stone walls, washed in amber light from hidden lanterns, seemed alive — ancient and watching. The sweeping drive curved like a serpent through manicured gardens, each twist lit by tiny ground lanterns flickering like fallen stars.

As Savannah's car crept forward, she leaned toward the window, wide-eyed. It was breathtaking. It was intimidating. It was everything she wasn't sure she was ready for. When the car finally rolled to a stop at the grand front steps, Vivian and Victoria Sinclair were already waiting.

Vivian was radiant in a dove-gray evening gown, a string of flawless pearls at her throat. Victoria stood beside her, wrapped in deep plum velvet, her posture straight, hands folded gracefully.

Vivian's smile was wide and gracious as she took Savannah's hands warmly. "My dear," she said, voice rich as molasses, "you look radiant." Victoria nodded slightly in agreement, her sharp gray eyes almost — almost — softening.

"You were the highlight of the last gathering," Vivian continued as she led Savannah inside. "Everyone spoke of you. So much promise. So much light."

Savannah blushed under the attention. "Thank you," she murmured, adjusting the strap of her dress nervously.

"And your studies?" Vivian asked as they passed through the towering entryway.

"Actually, yes. Professor Monroe invited me to join an advanced studies group." At that, both women exchanged a brief glance — quick, almost invisible — but Savannah caught it.

Vivian recovered instantly, her smile widening. "How wonderful," she said smoothly. "Such a rare honor. You must tell us all about it... someday." Something in her voice made Savannah's stomach tighten.

Before she could think too hard about it, Vivian swept open a set of double doors. And the world changed.

The dining room was a dream crafted from candlelight and music. A small round table sat near a wall of tall windows, overlooking the dark sweep of gardens beyond. The table was draped in crisp white linen, the center adorned with a simple, elegant bouquet of fresh gardenias. Candles flickered in crystal holders, throwing soft halos of light across polished silver and delicate china.

Soft strains of violin music floated through the air —
haunting, beautiful, almost sad.

And there, standing beside the table, was Jamie. He
wore dark slacks and a light gray shirt, sleeves casually rolled
to his elbows. When he saw her, his whole face lit up — not
the polite smile of obligation, but something real,
something rare.

"You look incredible," he said, his voice low and
sure.

Savannah laughed lightly, nerves melting under his
gaze. "So do you," she managed, cheeks flushing.

Jamie pulled out her chair with an easy grace. As she
sat, Savannah felt something settle around her —
something gentle and ancient, like stepping into a story that
had already been written long before she was born.

Dinner was exquisite. Rich pasta tangled with
fragrant herbs, bread so buttery it melted on her tongue,
crisp salads drizzled with sharp vinaigrette.

But Savannah barely tasted any of it. They talked.

And talked. And talked.

Jamie spoke of growing up feeling like an outsider — always chasing an expectation he couldn't name, trying to fill shoes that never quite fit.

Savannah shared her summers in the bayou — the smell of gardenias and gumbo, the slow swing of the porch hammock, the soft drone of cicadas at dusk.

They laughed over ridiculous childhood memories — Jamie's disastrous attempt at soccer, Savannah's failed spelling bee where she had misspelled "magnolia."

They mourned invisible scars — Jamie's sense of isolation, Savannah's aching loss of her parents.

At one point, Jamie leaned forward, his voice rough with something raw. "I feel like I've known you forever," he said. "Like you're the part I've been missing."

Savannah blinked rapidly, heart catching painfully in her chest.

She felt it too. Somewhere deep, beyond reason, beyond caution. Beyond fear.

After dinner, Jamie rose and held out his hand. Savannah took it without hesitation, feeling the warmth of his palm anchor her. He led her through the glass doors into the garden. The air was cool and thick with the scent of roses, lavender, and something older, wilder. Gravel crunched softly underfoot as they wandered through archways draped with vines, past marble fountains and ancient oaks strung with fairy lights. It was a dream spun of silver and shadows. At a small stone bench tucked beneath a weeping willow, they sat — still holding hands — gazing up at the endless stars. For a long, perfect moment, neither spoke.

Then — across the velvet sky — a single shooting star arched, brilliant and fast. Savannah gasped softly. "Make a wish," Jamie whispered against her hair. She closed her eyes. And wished. Not for fame. Not for fortune. But for this. For this feeling to last. When she opened her eyes again, Jamie was watching her with something naked and beautiful in his gaze.

The temperature dipped. Without hesitation, Jamie slipped off his jacket and draped it around her shoulders, his fingers brushing her arms in a touch so tender it almost broke her.

"Can't have you catching a cold," he said, smiling.

Savannah laughed — soft and aching — and leaned into him.

Above them, far above their fragile little world, the stars wheeled silently through the heavens. And above them, unseen, Jasper stood at an upstairs window. Watching. Seething. His fists clenched white-knuckled at his sides, teeth grinding in silent rage.

As they wandered back toward the mansion, laughter and music floated faintly from the grand windows. Savannah noticed a small group slipping up the front steps — Val and a few others from the lounge. Their energy was different tonight. Tight. Anxious. They offered polite smiles as they passed but didn't linger, disappearing into the house like whispered shadows.

Savannah hesitated at the base of the staircase. Through the archway, she glimpsed Vivian handing Val a folded slip of paper. "Blue hair. Blue dress. Tonight," Vivian said — her voice low, almost mechanical. Val's nod was robotic — tight, resigned. Savannah's stomach twisted. Something was wrong. Something was very wrong.

Later, slipping down a back hallway, Savannah caught sight of Val adjusting a newly dyed electric blue wig, smoothing a cheap blue dress over her body.

Savannah stepped forward. "Val... what's going on?"

Val startled, then flashed a brittle smile. "Vivian's just... Vivian," she said too brightly. "I owe her."

Savannah frowned, wanting to push, but Val squeezed her hand. "Don't worry about me," she whispered. "We'll talk tomorrow, okay?"

And then she was gone — swallowed by the night.

Jamie found her standing there, lost in thought. He slipped his arm around her, pulling her back into the present with a soft kiss to her temple.

"You okay?" he murmured.

Savannah nodded, leaning into him. More than

okay. Not perfect. Not safe. But somehow, with him, it felt bearable.

"Let me take you home," he said. "I'll have your car delivered tomorrow. I just... I don't want this night to end yet."

Neither did she.

The limo ride was a soft cocoon of velvet seats and whispered laughter. They talked in low voices, sharing silly confessions — favorite books, secret dreams.

Savannah fought the temptation to invite him inside when they reached her apartment building. Fought the pull of wanting — needing — more.

Jamie kissed her again, slow and deep and sure, his hand cupping her jaw like she was something precious. When they finally broke apart, he rested his forehead against hers. "Goodnight, beautiful," he whispered. "I'll call you tomorrow."

And he did not linger. He did not stay. He left her standing in the doorway, wrapped in his jacket, heart thrumming with hope and fear. Above her, the stars spun quietly, carrying secrets she could almost — but not quite — hear.

Interlude: Broken Chains, Invisible Cages

The city blurred past the black-tinted windows of the Cadillac Escalade, a wash of neon and shadow, life and lies. Val sat rigid in the backseat, arms folded tightly around herself, the scent of leather and expensive perfume coiling in the cold air like a noose.

Vivian always sent the best. Sleek. Pristine. Anonymous. The perfect chariot for missions like this — missions Val no longer allowed herself to name.

She pressed her forehead lightly against the glass, watching familiar streets slip past like ghosts. The ache inside her, heavy and hollow, never quite left anymore.

Tonight she wore a cheap, thin blue dress that clung to her like bruises she hadn't earned — a too-bright wig of electric blue hair perched awkwardly atop her head, itching against her scalp. In the reflection of the window, she could barely recognize herself.

Blue hair. Blue dress. Tonight. Vivian's instructions. Always so simple. Always so binding.

Her mind — traitorous, cruel — drifted back to the beginning. She had been thirteen. Just thirteen. Still young enough to believe that things could get better. Still foolish enough to believe in hope. She found her mother crumpled on the bathroom floor, arms limp, blood spattered against peeling tiles. The smell — chemical and sour and final — had made Val gag even as she screamed herself hoarse, shaking her mother's cold body until her own arms gave out. No one came. Not the neighbors. Not the city. Not God. No one ever came. The world simply turned its back and let her fall.

The streets swallowed her after that. She learned quickly. How to slip unseen through crowds. How to pick pockets without drawing a glance. How to trade the pieces of herself too small to miss — dignity, innocence, safety —

for warm beds and half-eaten meals. Sometimes her body. Sometimes her soul.

She became what the world demanded: ruthless. Hard. Forgettable. Until the day she picked the wrong target.

It was a bright afternoon — cruelly beautiful — the kind of day meant for children laughing, not children surviving. Val spotted her: An elegant woman in a silk scarf, leather gloves, and an air of absolute certainty. Easy mark. Val moved like a shadow through the crowded street, her hand brushing the smooth leather of the handbag. And froze.

It was like slamming into an invisible wall — an unseen force locking around her wrist, colder and harder than any police cuff. She gasped, trying to yank free. The woman turned. Vivian Sinclair.

No scream. No shout for help. Just a smile — slow, predatory, and almost affectionate. "As clever as you are lovely," Vivian had murmured, voice smooth as velvet and sharp as a blade. "Come with me, darling. Let's find you a better use."

The Escalade jolted sharply, jarring Val back to the present. Ahead of her, a second black SUV glided through the intersections, its headlights muted. Her friends — or what passed for friends — waited inside. Others scooped up from the streets over the years. Other lost things polished up and chained in silk. They followed Vivian's commands without hesitation. Just like Val. Because you didn't say no to Vivian Sinclair. You didn't break the chain — even when you couldn't see it anymore.

Val adjusted her wig mechanically, smoothing the cheap blue dress over her knees, forcing down the bile rising in her throat. There was no choice. There had never been a choice. Vivian had fed them, clothed them, protected them. And then she had bound them.

Not with law. Not with fear alone. But with ancient rites no one ever spoke aloud. With whispers. With relics. Loyalty disguised as salvation. Obedience disguised as love.

Sometimes Val wondered if she'd ever actually been free — even before Vivian found her. Sometimes she wondered if she was born in chains.

The Escalade slowed. They were here. A tall, narrow brownstone loomed above them — its windows dark, its stones cold even under the soft spill of streetlamps.

Val closed her eyes. Gathered herself. Get through it. Smile. Survive. She stepped out into the night, the hem of her dress whispering against the sidewalk.

The other car slipped into the shadows, her friends watching from a safe distance — ready to intervene if something went wrong. Not that it would matter.

Val climbed the stoop slowly, the blue of her dress flashing like a distress signal under the streetlights. She pressed the doorbell once — sharp, final.

The door opened almost immediately. Professor Adrian Monroe.

He wore no jacket. No smile. Just a cold, clinical stare — the kind that stripped flesh from bone without lifting a finger.

Val's stomach twisted into knots. There was no

misunderstanding. She wasn't here for conversation. She wasn't here for kindness. Vivian had delivered her — body and silence — wrapped neatly in loyalty she no longer recognized. Monroe stepped aside wordlessly.

Val crossed the threshold on shaking legs, leaving behind the stars, the night, and whatever thin, tattered hope she still harbored. The door closed behind her. The lock clicked into place. And the city forgot she had ever been there.

The sun was rising when she stumbled back into the street. The skyline burned gold against the cold gray of morning.

Val ripped the electric-blue wig from her head and hurled it into the nearest trash can, the fake hair twisting in the early breeze like broken wings.

Her heels were scuffed. Her mascara smeared raccoon-like shadows under deadened eyes. Her dress was torn at the hem. Her hands shook faintly as she pulled her jacket tighter around herself. She didn't cry. She hadn't cried in years. She just kept walking.

One step after another, shoulders hunched against the cold. Against the shame. Against the memory of hands she hadn't wanted. She wanted to go home. She wanted to sleep for a year. She wanted to wake up as someone else. Behind her, the city roared to life — blind, busy, indifferent.

Val melted into the morning haze, another broken ghost in a world that never cared enough to look closely. And the invisible leash around her throat pulled a little tighter.

Chapter 10: The Hands Behind the Veil

The morning light spilled lazily across Savannah's small apartment, casting long golden beams over the worn wooden floors and the half-opened boxes she still hadn't bothered to unpack.

She lay curled beneath a thick blanket, staring at the silent phone on her nightstand. Still no reply from Val.

Two days had passed since she last saw her — cheerful, hurried, disappearing into the New York night with her electric blue hair gleaming under the streetlights. Two days of silence.

Savannah told herself not to worry. Val was unpredictable. Free-spirited. Probably just busy. And yet... An uneasy hollowness coiled inside her chest, winding tighter with each passing hour.

She sighed and rolled onto her side — and her gaze caught on it. The journal. Still wrapped neatly in soft linen, resting atop the nightstand like a patient sentinel. Waiting. Calling. Today, she decided. Today, she would finally open it.

The coffee maker sputtered and hissed in the background, filling the tiny apartment with the rich, bitter scent of brewing warmth.

Savannah curled into the armchair near the window, a chipped mug balanced on the floor beside her, and carefully peeled back the linen cloth. The journal's leather cover was cool and smooth under her fingertips, worn soft by years of touch and travel. She opened it gently.

The first pages were filled with her grandmother's familiar handwriting — neat, looping cursive. Recipes for gumbo and pecan pralines. Notes about the tides and the weather. Short musings on the stubborn beauty of bayou gardens. A bittersweet ache bloomed in Savannah's chest.

But as she turned deeper into the journal, the tone

shifted. The handwriting grew tighter, more urgent. Cryptic phrases began to appear, scattered between mundane observations: "*There are hands behind the veil.*" "*Beware the golden smile.*" "*Gifts given too easily are rarely gifts at all.*"

There were sketches too — spirals, knotted circles, strange handprints etched with tiny symbols she didn't recognize. The longer she stared at them, the more they seemed to move at the edges of her vision, whispering secrets she couldn't quite hear. Savannah shivered and turned the page.

"*They weave unseen. They bind the young and the gifted without their knowledge. Beware.*"

A knock against the windowpane — a bird, just passing — jolted her upright. Her coffee had gone cold. She blinked down at the page, heart racing. Before she could dive deeper, her phone buzzed sharply on the nightstand.

A calendar alert flashed across the screen: Advanced Studies Group — North Hall, Room 512. Today.

Savannah glanced longingly back at the journal. Just one more thing, she told herself. One more obligation.

Then she would come back. She closed the journal gently and grabbed her bag.

North Hall was one of the oldest parts of the NYU campus — a crumbling, beautiful relic of dark wood paneling, dust-scented corridors, and creaking marble staircases.

Savannah's boots echoed sharply as she navigated the labyrinth of halls. Room 512 was at the end of a long corridor, tucked between heavy double doors worn down by generations of hands. She hesitated outside, nerves prickling under her skin. Then, steeling herself, she pushed the door open.

The room was dim and close. Old wooden tables stretched under low-hanging lights. Books piled in crooked towers against the walls. An ancient globe sat in one corner, its continents worn to watercolor smudges.

Seven students already filled the seats — older, sharper somehow than the ones she usually saw in her other classes. Their gazes flicked toward her as she entered, sizing her up in seconds, before turning away.

Professor Monroe stood at the head of the room, no lectern now — just a battered leather folio under his arm. He didn't smile. He never smiled. But when his pale, assessing gaze swept across the room and landed on her, something shifted. A faint, almost imperceptible nod. Approval. Recognition.

Savannah slid into a seat near the back, her heart pounding too loudly in her ears.

The session was not a lecture. It was a test. Monroe didn't speak in lessons. He spoke in riddles. Questions without answers. Challenges without maps.

He spoke of ancient bloodlines woven through centuries — hidden societies that protected their legacies not with armies, but with symbols, with vows, with blood rites whispered in the dark.

"Not all histories are written," he said, his voice low and threading through the dusky room. "Some are lived. Some are branded."

Savannah scribbled notes frantically, her pen sliding across the pages like a prayer. But the more she wrote, the more she realized... This wasn't just about the past. It was about now.

She caught small things out of the corner of her eye: A silver spiral ring on the finger of the girl next to her. A leather bracelet embossed with intricate sigils she recognized from her grandmother's journal. The way some students glanced at her when Monroe spoke of "those destined to awaken."

Her skin prickled. They knew something she didn't. And somehow, she was already woven into it.

After the meeting, as students packed up their notebooks and drifted out in tight, whispering clusters, Monroe approached her.

"You show great potential," he said, voice low, gaze steady.

Savannah flushed under the intensity of it. "Thank you," she murmured, clutching her bag tighter.

"If you stay the course," Monroe continued, "there are deeper studies. Doors few are ever invited to open."

Something about the way he said it made her shiver — part excitement, part dread. Before she could respond, another student sidled up, asking Monroe a question about research credit.

Monroe turned away without ceremony.

Savannah lingered a moment longer, uncertainty gnawing at her. Then she slipped out into the evening air.

The city felt different tonight. Sharper around the edges. The wind nipped at her cheeks as she made her way home, the shadows stretching long against the sidewalks.

When she finally tumbled into her apartment, she threw her bag aside and curled up on the couch, pulling the journal back into her lap. She flipped quickly to the page she had marked before.

"The hands behind the veil are rarely seen. They offer gifts — protection, love, power — but bind the soul beneath silk and gold. Few can break their hold once taken."

Her fingers trembled. Beside the passage was a sketched charm — a stone medallion carved with spirals.

The same kind she had seen locked in glass at the Sinclair estate. Coincidence? Or warning? The lines between history and prophecy blurred dangerously.

A knock shattered the stillness. Savannah jumped, her heart leaping into her throat. She crossed the small apartment cautiously and peered through the peephole. Jamie.

Standing there in a gray jacket, hair tousled from the wind, hands tucked into his pockets. When she opened the door, he smiled — tentative, hopeful.

"Hey," he said, his voice the only thing grounding her to the moment. "I couldn't stay away."

Savannah smiled, her heart leaping painfully. "Come in," she whispered.

He stepped across the threshold, bringing with him the scent of night air and something sweeter — something that wrapped around her like a promise. And as she closed the door behind him, the journal lay forgotten on the floor, whispering warnings she would not yet understand. Not yet. Not tonight.

Interlude: When the World Fell Away

Jamie entered, bringing with him the faint scent of rain and something sweeter — something that wrapped itself around her senses, dizzying and warm.

They moved instinctively toward the couch, sitting side by side — close enough that their knees brushed, close enough that their breaths tangled, but still holding back.

Still holding on. They talked, at first, because words were safer than silence. First kisses gone wrong. Embarrassing high school dances. Dreams of running away to places with names they couldn't pronounce.

Jamie spoke of sneaking onto the roof of his childhood home to watch meteor showers, wishing on every falling star for something he couldn't even name.

Savannah spoke of the heavy, humid summers in Louisiana — catching fireflies, the scent of her grandmother's gumbo thick in the air, believing for a little while that magic was real.

Their laughter softened into shared smiles. Their words slowed, thinning into a silence that was not awkward but charged — heavy with everything unsaid. Everything unavoidable.

Savannah shifted slightly, turning toward him. A lock of her hair slipped loose, falling across her cheek. Without thinking, Jamie reached out and brushed it back, his fingertips grazing the line of her jaw.

Savannah stilled under the light touch, breath catching. Their eyes locked. And the world — the apartment, the city, the past — fell away. There was only him. There was only her.

His hand lingered, cupping her cheek as if afraid she would vanish. She leaned into his touch without hesitation. And then, finally, finally, he kissed her.

The first kiss was feather-light, testing, tasting.

Savannah answered with a soft gasp, her fingers curling into the fabric of his shirt, pulling him closer. The kiss deepened — slow at first, then urgent, then consuming. She lost herself in it — in him — the weight of loneliness and hope crashing through her all at once.

Jamie responded, just as hungry — as if he had waited a lifetime for her — but there was a tremor beneath it. A restraint. A terrible, beautiful restraint.

It was Jamie who pulled back first, his forehead pressing against hers, his breath ragged. "God, Savannah," he whispered, his voice shaking with the force of everything he was holding back. "You have no idea how much I want you."

Her hands fisted lightly in his shirt. "Then don't stop," she whispered, her voice breaking.

Jamie squeezed his eyes shut, a muscle jumping in his jaw. "I have to."

Savannah blinked, confusion and hurt flashing across her face. "Why?"

When he opened his eyes, the look he gave her made her chest ache. Not rejection. Not hesitation. But a love so fierce it looked almost like pain.

"Because you deserve more than a moment," he said hoarsely. "You deserve forever. And if I let go now... I don't think I could ever stop."

Savannah bit her lip, tears threatening. She wanted to argue. Wanted to scream that she wanted him, needed him. But somehow, she understood.

Jamie wasn't pulling away because he didn't love her. He was pulling away because he did — more deeply, more desperately, than either of them could put into words.

"Then just..." Savannah's voice cracked. "Hold me."

Jamie's smile was small and reverent — like she had just given him something sacred. He pulled her into his arms without hesitation. She curled into him, tucking her head under his chin, her ear pressed over his heart. The steady, solid beat of it anchored her.

One of his hands stroked slow, soothing patterns

along her back, the other curling protectively around her waist. They stayed like that for a long time, the world outside fading into a distant hum. No words. No demands. Just presence. Just belonging.

Savannah drifted toward sleep, tucked into the shelter of him. In the fragile space between waking and dreaming, the words trembled on her lips: I love you. But she kept them safe inside her heart. Not yet. Not tonight.

She sighed against his chest, feeling the weight of loneliness lift — replaced by something terrifying and beautiful: Hope.

Outside the apartment, the city pulsed and roared, blind to the tiny, incandescent universe born in a second-floor walkup. Inside, under a threadbare blanket and a tangle of whispered promises, two broken souls stitched themselves quietly back together. One heartbeat at a time.

Chapter 11: Sails and Shadows

The morning sunlight streamed across Savannah's bed, warm and soft, stirring her awake. For a blissful moment, she smiled, eyes still closed, stretching her hand across the mattress to find Jamie's warmth beside her. But her fingers met only cool, empty sheets. Her smile faded slightly. Pushing herself up, she blinked against the light pouring in through the window. The apartment was quiet except for the familiar hum of traffic and distant horns — the restless heartbeat of New York City.

On the kitchen counter, something caught her eye: a folded piece of paper, tucked carefully under a coffee mug. Curious, Savannah padded over, the blanket wrapped around her shoulders like armor, and unfolded the note. *Didn't want to wake you. Last night was everything. I'll call you soon.*

— J.

She pressed the note against her chest, a small, bittersweet smile pulling at her lips. He hadn't stayed. But he hadn't vanished either. Still, the ache remained — a quiet, gnawing thing she couldn't name.

There was always a distance Jamie wouldn't cross. A shadow he wouldn't explain. What promise was he carrying alone? What secret weighed so heavily on him?

After a long, hot shower and a lazy cup of coffee, Savannah found herself curled on the couch, the leather journal cradled in her lap. The faded leather felt cool against her fingertips. She flipped past the opening pages, the cheerful garden notes, and recipes — deeper, deeper — until the handwriting grew sharper, the words heavier. "*Binding oaths, sworn before unseen witnesses, cannot be broken without grave consequence.*" "*Those chosen for sacred legacies are kept untouched, protected for purposes only revealed in time.*"

Savannah shivered, setting her coffee down, heart thudding. Was that what held Jamie back? Was he bound to something older, darker than she dared to imagine? It sounded insane.

And yet... She thought of the moments between them — the passion just barely restrained, the sorrow that clung to his silences. He loved her. She could feel it. But there were walls around him, walls built not from fear, but from duty. Walls she didn't know how to tear down.

A sharp knock startled her, jerking her from her thoughts. Savannah jumped up, clutching the journal protectively against her chest. Peeking through the peephole, she relaxed — but only slightly. It was Val.

Wearing oversized sunglasses and a leather jacket, her hair back to its familiar dark brown waves, Val bounced on her toes like nothing in the world could touch her. Savannah opened the door cautiously.

"Good morning, sleepyhead!" Val chirped, barging inside without waiting for an invitation.

Savannah blinked, caught off guard. "Where have you been? I've been worried."

Val shrugged, tossing her bag on the couch. "Life

got crazy, you know? Needed some air."

"You didn't answer any of my messages," Savannah said, trying to keep the hurt out of her voice.

Val's smile faltered for a half-second — a crack in her bright exterior — but she recovered quickly. "I know. I'm sorry, babe. Truly. But I'm fine. And today... today is about you."

Savannah hesitated, studying her friend closely. There was something different about Val — something tighter, sharper. But before she could press, Val clapped her hands and grinned.

"And guess what?" she said. "You're coming sailing with us!"

"Sailing?" Savannah repeated, skeptical.

"Yup! Sinclair's private yacht. You, me, sunshine, and bottomless champagne."

"I was kind of planning to stay in," Savannah said, thinking longingly of the journal waiting for her on the coffee table.

Val's smile dimmed, just a fraction. "Come on," she said, voice softening. "You need a day to just... breathe. Trust me."

Savannah hesitated. Something inside her — some cautious, buried voice — urged her to say no. But another part, the part that was tired of feeling alone, wanted to believe her friend. "Okay," she said finally. "One afternoon."

Val beamed, grabbing her hand. "You won't regret it."

Savannah smiled back, willing herself to believe it.

The Sinclair yacht was a floating dream. Sleek and gleaming under the midday sun, it cut through the water like a knife through silk. The sails billowed high overhead, snapping smartly against the bright blue sky.

Savannah stepped barefoot onto the warm teak deck, her hair whipping around her face in the salty breeze. For a little while, it was easy to forget everything.

Val danced to the thumping music blasting from

hidden speakers, dragging Savannah into laughter with ridiculous moves and inside jokes.

The other guests — beautiful, polished, vaguely familiar from the lounge — sipped champagne and shared lazy smiles like they owned the ocean.

Savannah tilted her face to the sun, letting the wind carry her worries away. She wanted to believe this was real. She wanted to believe she was finally living the life she deserved.

Curiosity eventually pulled her below deck. The yacht's interior was just as lavish as the estate — all gleaming white leather, polished wood, and golden fixtures.

Wandering through the softly lit hallways, Savannah stumbled upon a sideboard displaying framed photographs. She paused, drawn in. The first frame showed Vivian, vibrant and regal, steering the yacht with the kind of ease that spoke of generations spent mastering privilege.

The next photo punched the air from Savannah's lungs. Jamie and Jasper — younger, maybe twelve or thirteen. Dressed in matching navy shirts, standing stiffly side by side on the deck.

Jamie's grin was wide, easy — the same light she had fallen for.

But Jasper... Jasper's half-smile didn't quite reach his eyes. There was something coiled and restless behind his gaze — a resentment, a sadness.

It struck Savannah then — how long the distance between the brothers must have been growing, slow and silent like a crack beneath the surface. How many storms had been brewing, invisible, for years?

The afternoon stretched on in a golden haze. Savannah leaned against the rail, champagne in hand, watching the sun glitter on the endless water. Laughter drifted across the deck. Music pulsed low and steady. And yet... A quiet unease threaded through her.

Every so often, she thought of the journal tucked away at home. The relic she had seen at the Sinclair estate. The Binding Oaths. The hands behind the veil. She smiled, she laughed, she toasted the perfect day.

But inside, some small part of her knew: The tides were shifting. And no one drifted forever without eventually being pulled under.

Interlude: The Vow of Silence

The parlor was steeped in afternoon light, soft and gold through the heavy drapes. Vivian Sinclair sat perfectly poised on the velvet settee, a delicate porcelain cup balanced in one hand, her phone pressed against her ear.

She smiled — but the smile never touched her eyes. "Adrian," she said smoothly, her voice honeyed and calm, "you mustn't fret so."

On the other end of the line, Professor Monroe's voice was taut, almost panicked. "She's close to Valarie. If Val even hints at what happened that night — if Savannah connects the dots — everything could fall apart."

Vivian let out a low, indulgent laugh, twirling the cup in her fingers. "Valarie knows her place. Savannah is blissfully unaware. You have nothing to fear."

There was a beat of hesitation. "She's... extraordinary," Monroe said, the tension bleeding into something darker. "Savannah's intuition, her mind — she's different. I see higher aspirations for her. She could be... more than the others."

Vivian's smile thinned, a blade hidden behind silk. "You forget yourself, Adrian," she said quietly, each word a warning. "She is not like Valarie. She is not yours to claim. Treat her as a student — and nothing more."

A brittle pause crackled through the line. "Of course," Monroe said at last, his ambition tucked hastily back into obedience.

Vivian was about to dismiss him when the parlor doors swung open with a sharp click. Victoria Sinclair entered — precise, composed — a thin folder clutched in her hand. Vivian ended the call without a farewell and set the phone down lightly. "What is it, Victoria?"

Her sister crossed the room swiftly, her heels silent against the thick carpet. "Documents from the estate attorneys," Victoria said, her voice low, urgent.

Vivian arched a brow and opened the folder. Her gaze swept the neatly printed pages. Halfway through, she stilled — and then, slowly, a true smile bloomed. "He cannot inherit without marriage," she murmured, almost to herself. Her fingers tapped once, twice, against the parchment. "And the deadline is approaching."

Victoria inclined her head slightly. "We must act quickly."

Vivian closed the folder with a soft snap. "She must marry him," she said simply, as if it were already done.

That evening, the family gathered in one of the smaller salons — just Vivian, Victoria, Jamie, and Jasper. The room was cozy by Sinclair standards — dark oak walls, a low fire crackling in the hearth, heavy armchairs gathered around a Persian rug.

Jamie sat stiffly, his hands clasped between his knees. Jasper lounged against the fireplace, outwardly bored — but his sharp gaze missed nothing.

Vivian leaned forward, her tone velvet-soft but commanding. "You love her, don't you, Jamie?"

Jamie lifted his head slowly. His face — usually guarded — was open now, painfully raw. "I do," he said, voice low. "More than anything."

Victoria's cold gray gaze sharpened, assessing.

Vivian smiled, warm and victorious. "Then it's simple," she said. "You must marry her."

Jamie's shoulders tensed visibly. "I want to," he said, struggling, "but... she doesn't know everything. There's so much she doesn't understand about me. About us."

"In time," Vivian said gently, reaching across to cup his face in her hands — the gesture motherly, suffocating. "You will tell her in time."

Jamie's jaw clenched, eyes closing under the weight of it. "You don't understand," he said, voice rough. "If she knew... she might never—"

Vivian leaned closer, her voice soft and hypnotic. "My darling boy," she said, "trust me. Love will forgive many things. And once she is your wife, her heart will belong to you fully. There will be no turning back."

Jamie opened his eyes — and for a moment, anguish flared there, bright and terrible. But he nodded. Defeated. "I promise," he whispered.

Victoria exhaled softly, satisfied, her hands folding neatly in her lap.

Across the room, Jasper snorted — a harsh, bitter sound. "How nice for you," he muttered under his breath as he pushed away from the fireplace, stalking from the room like a shadow cut loose.

Vivian ignored him completely, her focus still locked on Jamie — her chosen son, her perfect pawn. She straightened, smoothing invisible wrinkles from her dress. "One step at a time," she murmured to herself.

Beyond the walls of the salon, deep within the bones of the house, the old magic stirred — restless, expectant. Waiting for the final knot to be tied. Waiting for Savannah Lacroix to step into the cage they had built for her.

Chapter 12:
Promises in the Air

The morning sunlight streamed through Savannah's kitchen window, warm and golden, pooling over the battered floorboards like liquid hope. She sat cross-legged at the kitchen table, lazily sipping her coffee, letting herself enjoy the rare quiet of a New York morning.

When her phone buzzed, she didn't jump. Somewhere deep inside, she already knew who it would be. She smiled even before she picked it up. Jamie. Dress comfortable. Trust me. Simple. Playful.

And somehow, it sent a thrill straight through her chest — sweeter than any love letter. Setting the phone down carefully, she leapt up from the table, laughing to herself. Today was already different. Today was already brighter.

An hour later, Jamie waited at the curb in a black SUV, leaning casually against the passenger door. He wore a crisp white button-down and jeans, his sunglasses pushed into the tousled dark hair she already adored.

The second he saw her, his face lit up in a grin — that half-boyish, half-devastating grin that turned Savannah's knees to water. "You look perfect," he said, opening the door for her with an effortless sweep.

Savannah laughed, slipping inside. "You haven't even seen what I'm wearing under the jacket."

Jamie smirked, sliding into the driver's seat. "I don't need to." And somehow, she believed him.

They drove for almost an hour, leaving the concrete and clamor of the city behind, the skyscrapers giving way to rolling green hills and tiny, sleepy towns. Savannah watched the world change outside her window, feeling like she was leaving her old life behind with every passing mile.

When they finally turned down a gravel lane and parked near a grove of swaying willows, she gasped. A small, sparkling lake glimmered at the center of the field, rowboats bobbing gently at the dock.

A checkered blanket was spread under the largest tree, with a massive wicker picnic basket perched beside it. It was like something out of a dream.

"You planned all this?" she asked, breathless.

Jamie shrugged, a little shy, a little proud. "Only the best for you."

Savannah could have cried. Instead, she laughed — pure, light, real.

The afternoon unfolded like a secret kept just for them. They ate sandwiches Jamie claimed to have made himself — though Savannah had her suspicions — and strawberries so sweet they stained her fingers red. They lay sprawled on the blanket afterward, the clouds drifting overhead like lazy ships, the sun slipping warm fingers across their skin.

Jamie reached for her hand without thinking, lacing their fingers together. "I used to think love was for other people," he said after a long while, his voice low, vulnerable. "Not for me."

Savannah turned her head, her heart aching at the raw honesty in his face. "But now?" she whispered.

He smiled — a small, soft thing. "Now I wonder if maybe it was waiting for me... if it was just waiting for you."

Tears pricked Savannah's eyes, but she blinked them away quickly, squeezing his hand instead. He didn't need words. He already knew.

Later, they rented a small rowboat and drifted into the center of the lake, the water glowing like molten gold under the setting sun. Savannah trailed her fingers along the surface, leaving tiny ripples behind them. Jamie leaned back, the oars forgotten in his lap, just watching her.

"I could see us building something beautiful

together," he said, almost to himself. "A home. A life that no one can take away."

Savannah sat up, turning to him fully. She saw it then — the fierce hope in him, the fear, the longing. She reached out and touched his cheek lightly. "I could too," she said, voice trembling slightly.

The look he gave her — part wonder, part devastation — nearly broke her.

The drive back was quieter, wrapped in the heavy, happy kind of silence that didn't need to be filled. Savannah leaned her head against the window, still holding Jamie's hand, memorizing the feeling of his thumb stroking lazy circles against her skin. She never wanted to forget this day. Not ever.

At her door, Jamie paused, his hands sliding up her arms, sending shivers across her skin. "I'm not rushing you," he said softly, brushing a strand of hair behind her ear. "No pressure. No expectations. Just... know that you're everything to me."

Savannah smiled, tears pressing against her throat.

"You too," she whispered.

He kissed her - slow, reverent, like a prayer whispered into the night. And then he pulled away, his forehead resting against hers for a lingering moment before stepping back. "I'll call you tomorrow," he promised. And this time, she believed he would.

Savannah leaned against the door after closing it, her heart racing, her cheeks flushed. For the first time, she let herself imagine it: A life built not out of survival, but out of choice. A marriage forged not out of duty, but out of fierce, impossible love. She smiled to herself, pressing her palms to the warm wood of the door.

Outside, the city settled into its night rhythm — lights blinking on, sirens keening faintly in the distance. Inside, Savannah whispered into the quiet: "Maybe... just maybe."

And far away — unseen, unnoticed — the invisible threads binding her future tightened ever so gently, the soft laughter of old magic carried on the wind. Waiting. Patient. Inevitable.

Chapter 13: A Future Promised

The morning sunlight painted Savannah's apartment in soft gold, and for once, she didn't rush. She moved barefoot through her tiny kitchen, humming under her breath, the coffee machine sputtering cheerfully. Life felt full in a way it hadn't since she was a child — before grief, before loneliness. It felt… right.

She caught herself daydreaming — imagining a future that stretched beyond classes and crowded sidewalks. A future with Jamie. Was it too soon? Maybe. But sometimes, the heart simply knew. She smiled into her coffee cup and allowed herself the dangerous, wonderful luxury of hope.

Across the city, Jamie sat rigid on a patio chair

behind the Sinclair mansion, the manicured gardens stretching endlessly before him. He hardly noticed the beauty. A crumpled letter sat crushed in his hand — a formal reminder from the estate attorneys. Neat. Inevitable. No inheritance without marriage. Deadline looming. Jamie ground the paper tighter in his fist. It wasn't the money that churned his gut. It was the secret. The shame.

The ancient chains wrapped around his soul that Savannah didn't even know existed. "She will forgive you once she loves you enough," Vivian's voice whispered in his mind.

He closed his eyes against the rising panic. He loved her. More than he thought possible. He just prayed — prayed until it hurt — that it would be enough.

In the Sinclair morning room, sunlight gleamed across polished wood as Vivian and Victoria sat surrounded by legal folders, sipping tea like generals before a campaign.

"She's blooming," Vivian said, flipping through reports from their watchers. "More trusting. More open. She's almost ready."

Victoria adjusted her spectacles, her gaze sharp. "Jamie has become compliant."

Vivian smiled — thin, knowing. "The soil is ready. It's time to plant the seed."

And they moved their pieces into place.

That afternoon, Valarie sat stiffly in Vivian's parlor, nodding as the orders were laid out with chilling precision. "Nothing overt," Vivian said smoothly. "A casual suggestion. A lovely place. A perfect place."

Val's stomach twisted, but she smiled and nodded. She always did. Deep down, a part of her screamed that Savannah deserved better. But she shoved it down. Like she always had. Obey. Survive. Forget.

The next day, Jamie paced his bedroom like a trapped animal. The small velvet box in his pocket felt like it weighed a thousand pounds. Inside was the ring — delicate, timeless, perfect for Savannah. He pulled it out, staring at it with trembling hands. "Please say yes," he whispered into the empty room. Not for the inheritance. Not for the legacy. But because without her, there was no future he wanted to live in.

At Savannah's apartment, Val played her part with a smile sharp enough to cut. They lounged on the couch, half-watching an old black-and-white movie.

"You know," Val said casually, swirling her wine, "there's this spot near Tarrytown. Private gardens, sunset views. So romantic. You and Jamie would love it."

Savannah tucked the thought away with a dreamy smile, never questioning it.

Val looked away quickly, guilt burning behind her eyes.

When Jamie picked Savannah up just before sunset, she was waiting in a soft sundress, her hair loose, her eyes bright. He couldn't stop staring. Couldn't stop memorizing her. She was the most beautiful thing he had ever seen — and maybe the last good thing he would ever have.

"You ready?" he asked, his voice rough with feeling.

"Always," she said, slipping her hand into his.

They drove in easy, sweet silence — the city melting

into open fields, the horizon painted gold and crimson.

The gardens were even more beautiful than Val had described. Winding stone paths disappeared into fields of wildflowers. The Hudson River glittered below like molten silver. The overlook — framed by weeping willows — stole Savannah's breath.

"It's beautiful," she whispered.

"Not as beautiful as you," Jamie said, and for once, he didn't care how cheesy it sounded. It was true.

They wandered slowly, laughing, teasing, sharing secret smiles. The weight of the world — the secrets, the plans, the old magic — seemed, for one perfect moment, to hold its breath.

At the edge of the overlook, Jamie stopped. Savannah turned — and froze. He was dropping to one knee. The bouquet of gardenias trembled in his hand. The setting sun wrapped him in gold. And in that moment, Savannah's world cracked open.

"Savannah Lacroix," he said, his voice unsteady but

sure, "you are the first person who made me believe in forever. The only home I've ever wanted. Will you marry me?"

Tears blurred her vision. Her heart thundered. For a second, she couldn't breathe — couldn't move — couldn't think. And then, somehow, the word found her lips: "Yes," she breathed.

And then, laughing through her tears, louder: "Yes! Yes!"

Jamie's hands were trembling as he slipped the ring onto her finger. He stood and caught her as she launched into his arms. Their kiss was sweet, fierce, desperate with joy. Around them, the world tilted — gardens spinning, rivers sparkling, stars beginning to pierce the darkening sky.

Savannah didn't see the invisible strings weaving tighter around her heart. Didn't hear the faint, triumphant whisper from far away, carried on the wind. She only saw Jamie.

And Jamie — broken, bound, desperate — only saw her. The girl who had become his entire salvation. The girl he would fight heaven and hell to protect. Even if it cost him everything.

Chapter 14: The Second Ceremony

The morning sunlight spilled like liquid gold across Savannah's bedroom, warming the pale walls and curling into the corners where unopened gifts still sat in neat, waiting piles. She twirled slowly before the mirror, the folds of her ivory dress catching and scattering the light like pieces of a dream she wasn't quite ready to wake from.

For a heartbeat, she was a little girl again — barefoot in the bayou mud, a crown of daisies crooked in her hair, whispering promises to a future she hadn't yet dared to believe she deserved.

"One day," she had sworn to the empty fields. "One day, I'll find love that stays." Today, it felt like she had.

The wedding had been everything she had ever

imagined and more. A soft ceremony lit by thousands of tiny candles. Towering bouquets of white roses perfumed the air. Laughter drifted like music across the manicured lawn. She remembered the way Jamie had looked at her — as if she were the only thing that existed in the world. Their friends had clapped and cheered as they danced, spinning slowly beneath a ceiling of stars. Even strangers, drawn into the orbit of the Sinclair wealth and legacy, had smiled at them — a sea of shimmering faces, champagne glasses raised in joyful benediction.

It was a dream. It was her dream. And yet... Somewhere, faintly, a wrong note had hummed beneath the perfect melody.

Across the sprawling halls of the Sinclair estate, the air had thickened. In the study, the true ceremony had been prepared. Vivian and Victoria hovered like twin specters over the ancient relics laid reverently on the heavy mahogany table. A silver chalice — carved with symbols that should not have been remembered. A braided cord of black and gold — humming faintly with old magic. An obsidian pendant — cool, dark, and hungry. The Second

Ceremony. The true binding. The final tether that would seal Savannah's fate to the Sinclair legacy — body, mind, and soul.

Vivian smoothed the folds of her gown, satisfaction glinting in her ice-pale eyes. Everything was aligned. Savannah's heart was full — open — vulnerable. She would never even know what had been taken from her until it was too late.

A soft knock at the door shattered the moment. Victoria opened it — expecting obedience, perhaps a servant announcing the bride's arrival. Instead, Jamie stood framed in the doorway, still in his tuxedo, his jaw clenched tight with the force of the decision he had made.

"We won't be staying," he said simply.

Victoria blinked, unaccustomed to being disobeyed.

Vivian rose slowly from her chair, the picture of perfect, poisonous grace. "And why ever not, darling?" she purred.

Jamie met her gaze head-on. "I bought a house," he

said. "A place for Savannah and me to start our life. Tonight. Together."

Silence exploded into the room like a thunderclap. A candle guttered. The silver chalice trembled faintly on the table. Vivian's smile didn't falter — but her eyes gleamed, sharp and cold. "Running won't change destiny," she said, voice as soft as silk, as deadly as steel.

Jamie said nothing. He simply turned and walked away. The click of the closing door sounded like a gunshot.

Vivian's smile withered into a thin, furious line.

Victoria's lips peeled back in a snarl. "Foolish boy."

Vivian's knuckles whitened around the silver chalice. "Then we wait," she said coldly. "And we adapt."

The house Jamie had bought was nothing like the estate. It was smaller — humbler — but to Savannah, it felt like stepping into a secret garden carved just for them. Warm wood floors. Wide sunlit windows. Gardens thick with roses and ivy. It was imperfect. It was perfect.

Jamie carried her over the threshold, laughing as she

squealed and clung to him. "You're the most beautiful thing I've ever seen," he whispered, setting her gently down.

Tears pricked Savannah's eyes. "If this is a dream," she said, her voice trembling, "I don't ever want to wake up."

Their kiss was slow, reverent — full of unspoken promises. For a moment, she believed with all her heart that their love would be enough to rewrite whatever stories fate had once etched into the stars.

But then Jamie's mood shifted. Gently, he pulled back, taking her hands between his. His palms were rough and warm and trembling faintly. "I need to tell you something," he said.

Savannah's heart stuttered.

Jamie's eyes darkened, shadowed with something heavy and terrible. "I love you," he said hoarsely. "More than anything. More than I even know how to say." "But because I love you... we're going to have separate rooms."

The words hit her like a stone to the chest.

Savannah stared at him, confused and aching. "But why?" she whispered.

Jamie swallowed hard, his fingers tightening slightly around hers. "There are things I have to protect you from," he said. "Even from myself." "Please, Savannah... please trust me."

She searched his face — every line, every shadow — looking for answers she couldn't find. He pressed a kiss to her forehead — tender, sorrowful. "You've already given me everything," he whispered against her skin. "I can wait for the rest."

Savannah nodded, her throat burning. Because what else could she do? She loved him. She would always love him. Even if she didn't understand the walls he was building between them.

Her bedroom was beautiful — ivory linens, soft gray walls, fresh roses blooming in a glass vase. It was a princess's room. But to Savannah, it felt like exile. She curled under the thick covers, staring at the ceiling. Her wedding ring caught the moonlight, flashing cold and bright. She twirled it slowly, over and over, the silver band glinting with each twist.

She wanted to believe Jamie. Wanted to believe that this distance was love, not rejection. But doubts whispered to her in the dark. Had she done something wrong? Was there something broken in her that he had seen and pulled away from? Or — worse — was there something broken in him? Something no amount of love could ever fix?

Outside her window, the garden roses bowed under the kiss of the night wind. Inside, Savannah lay awake, her heart splintering quietly beneath the weight of unanswered questions. And somewhere deep within the old city, the hands behind the veil stirred, weaving threads tighter around the dream she thought was hers to keep.

Chapter 15: The Cage of Love

The late morning sun spilled lazily across the floors of the new house Jamie had bought for them — warm, golden, almost too bright for the heavy knot twisting in Savannah's stomach.

Savannah stood in the center of the living room, barefoot, arms crossed, watching as the movers finished unloading the last battered boxes from her old life.

It should have made her feel... triumphant. Whole. Instead, a hollow ache gnawed at the corners of her heart. The life she had built — all those fragile pieces of herself — now sat crammed into neat, sterile stacks against the walls of a house that was beautiful, but not yet hers.

After the movers left, she wandered through the

boxes, tugging at old tape seams, letting memories spill out. Books. Framed photos of smiling parents frozen in time. A faded Mardi Gras mask from her last true summer of childhood. Tiny, ridiculous trinkets that had survived too many moves.

And then she found it. A small box, worn soft by years of hands, labeled in her grandmother's delicate script: Personal. Her breath caught as she knelt, heart hammering. Inside, wrapped carefully in an old linen shawl, was the leather journal. The one she had promised herself she would read. The one she had feared. Today, she could run no longer.

She curled into the sun-warmed sitting nook of their bedroom, legs tucked beneath her, the journal cradled on her knees like a fragile creature. The wide windows let in the spring breeze, carrying the scent of the new garden Jamie had planted for her — roses, gardenias, jasmine. A garden meant for dreams.

But Savannah could no longer ignore the shadows creeping beneath its beauty. She flipped to the worn page she had marked. "Binding oaths, sworn before unseen witnesses, cannot be broken without grave consequence." "Those chosen for sacred legacies are kept untouched, protected for purposes only revealed in time."

Her voice shook as she read it aloud, the syllables cutting through the bright air like knives. Over and over, she spoke the words — until something inside her began to hum, low and uneasy, like a harp string stretched too tight.

Images flickered behind her closed eyelids — silver cords tightening around wrists, ancient hands weaving threads into blood and bone, names whispered over cradles before memory could even form.

She shivered violently and closed the journal, pressing it to her chest. Love. She had love now. And she would fight for it. No matter what shadows stirred.

The days blurred, strange and beautiful in equal measure. Jamie adored her. There was no mistaking that. Each morning she woke to find breakfast prepared with almost reverent care — fresh berries shaped into hearts, buttery croissants still warm from the oven.

Little love notes tucked into her pockets: "You are my North Star." "I exist because you breathe." "Forever is too short with you."

He kissed her forehead before leaving for his charity work each day, his hand lingering at her waist just a moment longer than necessary. To the world, they were a perfect picture of newlywed bliss. But inside their home, inside her heart, cracks were beginning to form. Cracks Jamie refused to see.

She craved him. Not just his touch — though God, how she missed it — but the closeness, the full surrender of hearts and bodies promised in wedding vows. But every advance, every tender reaching, was gently — painfully — rebuffed.

Jamie locked the bathroom door when he showered. He changed behind closed doors. He brushed off her tentative touches with strained smiles and murmured excuses. And always — always — that wall between them grew taller.

And then, the dreams began.

The first dream was so vivid Savannah woke up sobbing, gasping for breath.

She was a teenager again, huddled in the back seat of her father's old pickup truck. Rain lashed the windows in furious sheets, the windshield wipers squealing uselessly against the flood. Her mother sat stiffly in the passenger seat, clutching the dashboard with white knuckles. "Slow down, David!" she cried, voice sharp with fear. "Please, the storm—!" Her father, tense and grim, hunched over the wheel, stubbornly pushing forward into the darkness. Outside, lightning split the sky — and for a flash, Savannah saw it. On the dashboard — in a pocket tucked near her father's hand — a strange object gleamed. A relic. Something carved with spirals, dark and ancient, not belonging to them. Her mother screamed. The truck jerked violently — hydroplaning, spinning — and then there was impact. A sickening crunch of metal and glass. Then darkness.

Savannah woke clawing at the sheets, drenched in sweat. A scream tore from her throat before she could stop it. Jamie was there in an instant, hauling her into his arms, rocking her gently. "It's okay, love," he whispered over and over, stroking her damp hair. "I'm here. You're safe."

She sobbed against his chest, the weight of the dream — or memory? — crashing down on her. Her parents. Their accident. She had always believed it was just that — a tragic, senseless accident. But now... Was it? Or had something older, something darker, twisted fate that night?

Jamie stayed with her until her breathing slowed, until sleep tugged at her again. But by morning, as always, he was gone. Only a fresh breakfast tray and a single white gardenia waited for her on the nightstand.

The dreams returned again and again. Sometimes she found herself back in that truck — screaming for her parents as rain blinded her. Other nights she wandered through a dense, mist-shrouded forest, barefoot, her white nightgown trailing behind her like a ghost. Somewhere ahead, someone called her name.

"Savannah... Savannah..."

But when she ran toward it, a silver cord snapped

tight around her wrist, yanking her backward. No matter how hard she pulled, she could not move. Above her, shadowed faces floated — eyeless, voiceless — murmuring a single word:

"Handler. Handler. Handler."

She woke sobbing, the sheets tangled around her like chains. Jamie was there in an instant. He gathered her into his arms without a word, rocking her against his chest, his heart hammering wildly beneath her cheek. "Shhh, love," he whispered over and over. "I'm here. You're safe."

She clung to him like a drowning woman, and slowly, eventually, she slipped back into sleep cradled in his arms. But when she woke the next morning, he was gone. Only a tray of fresh fruit and coffee waited — a single gardenia laid atop the linen napkin.

Night after night, it happened. The dreams grew darker, sharper. Tangled cords. Symbols burning behind her eyes. A sense of being watched by something immense and ancient and cold.

Every night, Jamie came. Held her. Soothed her.

Loved her without ever truly touching her. And every morning, he disappeared.

One morning over breakfast, Savannah finally found the courage to speak. Her voice shook. "Jamie... these dreams. They feel..." she hesitated, searching for the right word, "real. Important. Like warnings."

Jamie looked up from his coffee slowly, his face shuttered. "It's just stress," he said with careful gentleness. "The wedding. The move. Your studies. It's a lot." He reached across the table, squeezing her hand. "Maybe it's time to take a break from the University," he suggested.

Savannah stared at him, stunned. Her studies were everything she had left of herself — the only thing she had ever claimed without compromise. To give that up... She swallowed her protest, feeling the first true seed of fear root itself in her heart.

The days grew heavier. Jamie treated her like a queen — yes — but it was a love wrapped in velvet chains. He kissed her forehead but not her mouth. He held her hand but not her body. He left poetry scrawled on napkins but locked doors between them at night. Savannah was drowning in sweetness. And starving for the truth.

Some nights, lying awake in the vast coldness of their shared — but divided — home, Savannah thought about leaving. Not because she didn't love him. Because she loved him too much to pretend everything was enough. Jamie was hiding something. And love without truth was no love at all. But because love, when built on silence and half-truths, felt less like freedom… and more like a gilded cage. Beautiful. Golden. Deadly.

Chapter 16: The Final Weaving

The candles burned low in the Sinclair mansion, the heavy air thick with ancient scents — sandalwood, crushed petals, and something sharper underneath — old ash and binding smoke.

Vivian moved carefully around the black-lacquered table, her fingers brushing reverently over the relics assembled there. Small objects. Innocuous to the untrained eye. But in truth, each one a weapon — designed to break will, to twist dreams, to bind love until it became a noose.

Victoria stood nearby, clutching a velvet pouch tight against her chest. "Place them where the heart beats strongest," Vivian said, her voice almost a purr.

Victoria nodded once, and the two women began

their grim work — weaving a net invisible to the naked eye, a trap Savannah would never even see.

At dawn, while the city still slept and the mist clung low to the sidewalks, their agents moved. Among them — Valarie. Her hands shook slightly as she slipped through the halls of Savannah's house, her boots making no sound against the polished wood floors. Behind mirrors. Under beds. Buried shallowly in the garden soil. Tucked inside old books Savannah loved. The relics were hidden — woven into the very bones of the house, whispering through the air, clinging to every surface like smoke.

When Savannah returned from her morning errands, she paused on the threshold. The house felt different. Heavier. Darker. As if unseen eyes now tracked her every movement.

At first, Savannah told herself it was nothing. Stress. Fatigue. The adjustment to married life. But the strangeness became impossible to ignore. Mirrors she hadn't touched cracked in spiderweb patterns overnight. Books fell from shelves she hadn't approached. Cold drafts whispered through sealed windows. Fresh flowers wilted and died within hours of being placed. Even her wedding bouquet — white gardenias Jamie had so tenderly chosen — blackened at the edges as if touched by unseen flames. And at night... The dreams grew darker.

Again, Savannah was back in the passenger seat of her father's battered pickup truck. Rain battered the windows so hard she could barely see beyond the streaking glass. She was a teenager again — skinny, awkward, still half-believing that love could conquer everything. Her mother clutched the dashboard, her face pale with fear. "Slow down, David!" "Please — it's not safe!" Her father's jaw was set, his hands white-knuckled around the steering wheel. Through the downpour, something flashed — not lightning, but something inside the truck. Something tucked near her father's side. Savannah caught a glimpse: A small, spiral-carved relic. Ancient. Familiar. Its presence made the air hum, thick with dread. And then — a skid. a scream. a sickening impact that ripped the world apart. When she crawled from the wreckage, blood in her mouth and glass in her hair, her parents lay still. Silent. Gone.

Savannah jerked awake with a ragged sob, heart hammering against her ribs. The dream clung to her like a second skin — so vivid she could still smell the burning rubber and rain.

Jamie was there in an instant, his arms wrapping around her, his voice soft and desperate against her ear. "I'm here, love." "You're safe." "You're safe." But was she? Or had she ever been? Every night after, the dreams returned — twisting. Reaching.

Some nights, she ran endless corridors lined with mirrors that didn't reflect her. Other nights, she floated through heavy mist while unseen hands wove silver cords around her wrists, pulling her down, down, down— Handler. Handler. Handler. The whispered word echoed in her ears long after she woke.

Jamie fought back in silence. Night after night, when Savannah finally collapsed into exhausted sleep, he scoured the house. He found the relics one by one — hidden behind paintings, inside vents, sewn into the seams of her clothes. Each object pulsed with a sick, malevolent energy. Each one was a poison meant to bleed her dry without a single wound.

Jamie destroyed them in secret — smashing, burning, burying the remnants in the woods far beyond the property line. But it was never enough. Every time he removed one, another appeared. He could feel the net tightening around them. And he knew — time was running out.

Across the city, inside the cold, immaculate halls of the Sinclair estate, Vivian and Victoria waited. "It isn't working," Victoria snarled, pacing like a cornered wolf. "Something is interfering."

Vivian merely sipped her tea, unbothered. "The bindings are ancient. They cannot be undone by will alone." "Eventually, she will break." Her lips curled into a predatory smile. "Love is the cage she built herself."

Meanwhile, Savannah's heart was unraveling. She sat with Jamie one twilight evening, the garden fading into blue shadows around them, the scent of damp roses filling the air. Her hands twisted restlessly in her lap, the wedding ring catching the last light of day. Finally — when she couldn't hold it inside anymore — she turned to him.

"Jamie..." she whispered. Her voice cracked. "I love you more than anything. But... I can't live like this anymore."

Jamie froze, staring at her as if the earth had opened beneath his feet.

She swallowed hard, blinking against the tears she refused to shed. "If you can't trust me — if you can't open your heart to me fully — then maybe... maybe we were never meant to be."

The silence between them shattered something sacred. Jamie's face crumpled — truly, completely — as if she had torn out the last piece of him. He opened his mouth. Closed it. Opened it again. Tears burned in his eyes. But he said nothing.

Savannah stood, every step away from him like tearing off pieces of herself. "I need the truth," she whispered, voice breaking. "I deserve the truth."

That night, long after Savannah's tears had soaked into her pillow, Jamie sat alone on the back porch, his head bowed. The moon hung heavy and judgmental above him. The box he had hidden for so long — the truth — pulsed against his chest. If he spoke, he would lose her. If he stayed silent, he would lose her anyway. Jamie buried his face in his hands and wept — the broken, soundless sobs of a man who knew he had already lost the only thing that ever truly belonged to him.

Tomorrow, he decided. Tomorrow, he would tell her everything. And if it destroyed them both — so be it.

Chapter 17: The Shattered Vow

The night pressed heavy around them, thick with the scent of roses — and something deeper, older. A sorrow that clung like mist to the stones of the garden. Savannah sat silent on the bench, the moonlight catching the folds of her white nightdress, turning her into something ethereal. Her hands were knotted tightly in her lap, the wedding ring glinting cold on her trembling finger.

Jamie stood a few feet away, his back to her, rigid as stone. The shadows clung to him, blurring the edges of his tall frame as if the night itself tried to pull him under. A long, aching silence.

Savannah's heart thudded painfully in her chest, each beat a question she was too afraid to ask.

Finally — Jamie turned. And in the silvered light, she saw it: the devastation. His face was pale and drawn, his eyes glittering with unshed tears, his hands trembling uselessly at his sides.

He opened his mouth — Closed it. And then — slowly — he dropped to his knees before her. "I should have told you the moment I met you," he said, his voice low and shredded with grief. "I should have run... or begged you to run."

Savannah stared, too stunned to move.

"I never deserved you," Jamie whispered, voice breaking. "Everything I did — every lie, every silence — it was to protect you."

Savannah's breath hitched, her pulse roaring in her ears. "Protect me from what?" she asked, barely a breath.

Jamie bowed his head. For a moment, it seemed like the whole world held its breath. "I'm not..." he started — stopped — tried again. "I'm not an ordinary man."

Savannah's hands clenched tighter.

Jamie closed his eyes. And the memories came, flooding back in jagged flashes: He was a boy again — seven years old, standing in the cold marble halls of the Sinclair estate, his hand locked tightly in Jasper's. The ceremony room had smelled of burning herbs and iron and blood. Vivian's voice — soft, sweet, deadly — had promised them greatness. "You're special, my darlings. Chosen. Blessed."

Jamie remembered the cold touch of the relic pressed to his bare skin. The sudden, searing pain. The way Jasper had cried out — a sound that still haunted Jamie's nightmares. They had carved the futures into them with knives and oaths before either boy could understand what was being stolen.

Jamie's voice shook as he forced himself back to the present.

"Vivian. Victoria." Their names tasted like ash in his mouth. "They aren't just guardians. They are Handlers — part of a line older than even they remember. Born to influence, raised to manipulate, they don't just protect legacies — they craft them. They choose heirs, shape destinies, and bind power to bloodlines not their own. Always from the shadows. Always behind the throne. Their charge was once sacred, a gift. But somewhere through the centuries, they began to believe the legacies belonged to them. And now? Now they don't serve power. They hoard it."

Savannah flinched, shaking her head slightly as if to ward off the words. "You and Jasper..." she whispered.

Jamie nodded, shame burning through him. "They chose us. Broke us. Used relics to bind us before we even knew what choice was." His fists clenched against his thighs. "They cut away everything that could defy them."

Savannah frowned, confusion flickering across her tear-streaked face.

Jamie swallowed — hard — and the next words ripped out of him like broken glass. "We were castrated."

Savannah recoiled, a strangled gasp escaping her.

Jamie couldn't meet her eyes. "When I told you we needed separate rooms..." his voice cracked. "It wasn't because I didn't want you. God, Savannah, I wanted you more than breath." "But they... they made sure I never could."

The garden blurred into shadow and mist. Savannah covered her mouth, her mind reeling. It was too much. Too cruel. Too monstrous to be real.

"They tattooed us too," Jamie said hollowly. "Ranked us. Marked us."

Savannah remembered — the tiny '1' inked between Jamie's thumb and forefinger. The '2' on Jasper's.

"I was marked the Heir," Jamie said, a bitter twist to his mouth. "Meant to marry. Meant to claim. Meant to bind bloodlines the way they demanded." He lifted his head finally, eyes burning. "And you —" he whispered, "you were the final piece. The golden girl. The inheritance. The victory they were waiting for."

Savannah's whole body shook with the force of the revelation. "So it was never about me," she said numbly. "It was about my blood."

Jamie's face crumpled. "No," he said urgently. "I didn't know — not at first. I swear to you." He crawled closer on his knees, desperate. "When I met you at the coffee shop... you were just Savannah. Bright, fierce, breathtaking Savannah. You made me feel... alive. Like I was more than their puppet."

Tears ran down Savannah's cheeks unchecked. "Then why didn't you tell me? Why keep me trapped in a lie?"

Jamie's hands shook violently. "Because the truth would have destroyed you." "Because I didn't know how to live if you left."

Silence crushed them.

Jamie dropped his gaze, his voice raw. "Every night I fought them," he whispered. "Every night I destroyed what they sent — relics, spells, bindings hidden in the house." "They tried to weave you into their web... and I fought. God, I fought."

Savannah stared at him, tears blurring her vision.

"And I knew..." Jamie's voice dropped lower, shaking. "I knew eventually I'd lose."

He lifted his gaze to hers — and she saw it. The boy who had been broken. The man who had tried, hopelessly, to put the pieces back together. The man who had loved her with a love born of ashes and ruin.

"I love you," Jamie said, voice ragged. "I loved you before I even knew what love was supposed to mean." "If you walk away," he said, his voice breaking, "I won't stop you." He pressed his forehead to the ground before her feet — the old, ancient gesture of surrender. "I just needed you to know the truth."

Savannah sat frozen, the ring heavy on her hand, her heart a shattered thing inside her chest. The man she loved knelt before her — stripped of every lie, every armor, every hope. Tears slid down her cheeks silently. And for the first time, she realized — He had loved her with everything he had left. And still, maybe, it wouldn't be enough to save them. Not from the sins of the past. Not from the ghosts binding them both. Not even from each other.

Chapter 18: Savannah's Choice

Jamie cried himself to sleep. He hadn't wept like that since he was a boy — a broken child on cold marble floors, begging hands that would never hold him with love.

Now, curled alone in his room on his hollow bed, he sobbed for the only person who had ever made him believe he was more than what he had been created to be. Savannah.

The night stretched long and merciless, and when morning finally clawed through the windows, Jamie bolted upright, heart hammering. The house was too quiet.

He stumbled from the bed, barefoot, frantic, checking the closet, the drawers. Her clothes were still there. Her books. Her scent lingering on the sheets. But

Savannah was gone.

The mist rolled in heavier as Savannah walked the city streets, her boots splashing through shallow puddles, her hands stuffed deep into her coat pockets. Morning blurred into afternoon, and still she wandered — past shuttered storefronts, past the drifting smells of bakeries and coffee shops, past the laughing clatter of strangers' lives carrying on without her. The cold bit into her skin, threading under her clothes, numbing her fingers, her face. She barely noticed.

Everywhere she walked, memories followed. Jamie's laugh — soft and rare — when she told a terrible joke. The way he pressed his forehead to hers when he thought she might cry. The countless nights he had held her while she slept, never asking for anything in return.

Now, all those memories twisted inside her — new, raw, refracted through the terrible truth he had confessed. Had any of it been real? Or had she loved a ghost spun by someone else's cruel hand?

The ache in her chest grew sharper with every step.

She remembered her grandmother's voice, soft and grave: "Beware the hands behind the veil, child. They weave what the heart cannot see."

Savannah pulled her coat tighter, the fabric rough against her fingertips. Her breath fogged the cold air, each exhale a visible testament to her indecision.

She thought she had known herself — strong, steady, cautious. But Jamie had shattered her. He had made her reckless. He had made her want.

She reached the riverside just as the sun began to slip behind the buildings, painting the mist in bruised purples and grays. The city hummed distantly behind her — the muted wail of sirens, the rhythmic clatter of passing trains, the lonely bark of a dog. The world kept turning. No matter what choice she made.

She sat on a wet bench and let the cold soak through her jeans, staring blindly at the churning river. Jamie hadn't lied because he wanted to hurt her. He had lied because he was afraid.

Afraid that if she knew the ugly truth — the broken

truth — she would run. Savannah closed her eyes. Could she live with what had been done to him? Could she live without him? Her hand drifted to her wedding ring, twisting it slowly. Not perfect. Not easy. But real. Real in a way nothing else had ever been.

The mist thickened as darkness fell. Savannah rose slowly, her knees stiff, her body aching. She turned toward home — toward the house that had become both a sanctuary and a prison. Toward him.

The house loomed in the mist, its windows glowing softly against the night. Inside, it was silent. Savannah slipped in quietly, leaving her damp coat by the door.

The air smelled like home — cedarwood, rain, and the faintest lingering trace of Jamie's cologne. She moved through the house like a whisper, past the living room, the kitchen, the stairs. No sign of him. Her heart twisted painfully.

She climbed the stairs slowly, hand trailing the polished wood banister. At the top landing, she paused. Two doors. Hers. And Jamie's. Both closed.

Her hand shook as she reached for her door. Inside, everything was as she had left it — the untouched bed, the journal resting on the nightstand, the windows rattling faintly with the rising wind. For a long moment, she just stood there — caught between the life she had lived, and the one she would choose.

Finally, she turned — and crossed the hallway to Jamie's door. Her hand hovered at the handle, her heart hammering so hard it made her ears ring. On the other side of that door was the man who had loved her with every broken, desperate piece of himself. The man who had never once asked her for more than she was willing to give.

Savannah pressed her palm to the door — felt the faint thud of her own pulse against the cold wood. Slowly, she opened it.

Jamie lay curled on the bed, fully clothed, his body a tight knot of grief. Tear tracks stained his cheeks. One hand was clenched loosely around a crumpled piece of paper — a letter she would never have to read to know what it said. Goodbye. I'm sorry. I love you.

Savannah stepped into the room, silent. She crossed the floor and knelt beside him. For a moment, she just watched him — the broken boy who had become the man she loved more than breath itself. Then, with infinite tenderness, she reached out and touched his hair.

Jamie stirred — and when he opened his eyes and saw her there, he flinched, as if afraid the sight of her was just another cruel dream.

Savannah smiled through her tears. "No more walls," she whispered. "No more lies." "But if I stay," she whispered, pulling back to look at him, "you must cut them off. Vivian. Victoria. All of them. Forever."

Jamie nodded without hesitation, his voice breaking. "I already have." Jamie shook his head desperately, broken words falling from his lips. "I'm sorry — I'm so sorry — I should have told you — I should have run —"

She silenced him with a kiss — soft, aching — pressing every ounce of forgiveness and fury and love she had into the touch of her mouth against his.

When she pulled back, he was weeping openly. "I choose you," Savannah said fiercely, framing his face with her hands. "I choose you, Jamie Sinclair. No matter the past. No matter the scars. No matter the chains they tried to wrap around us."

Jamie crumpled into her arms, sobbing like a man who had finally found his way home. And Savannah held him — held them both — together.

Outside, the mist howled against the windows. The old hands behind the veil tugged and wove in fury. But inside the battered heart of their little home — love rewrote fate.

Chapter 19: The Vow Reclaimed

She touched his face, and for the first time in weeks, they smiled — broken, battered, but smiling. "Then take me," she whispered. "Not because of them. Not because of fate. Because you love me."

They made their way to her bedroom that had felt too big, too empty for too long.

Jamie closed the door softly behind them, then turned to face her. He swallowed hard, his hands shaking. Slowly, he began to undress — piece by piece — stripping away not just his clothes, but the lies, the shame, the chains. His body bore the scars of a life stolen — jagged lines across his sides, a faint but cruel surgical mark hidden low along his abdomen. He stood naked before her, trembling with vulnerability. No woman had ever seen him like this.

Savannah crossed to him without hesitation. Tears filled her eyes — but not from pity. From love. From fierce, blinding love. She touched his chest, feeling the wild stammer of his heart. "You are beautiful," she said. And he believed her.

That night, they did not make love in the way stories promised. They made love in every other way. Jamie kissed her — slow, aching kisses — like she was a prayer he didn't deserve to speak aloud. They moved together in the dim candlelight, the world shrinking to the fragile space between them. Jamie kissed her slowly — lingering kisses pressed to her lips, her cheeks, her throat — as if memorizing her piece by precious piece. His hands skimmed along her sides, trembling slightly, and when he reached the hem of her nightdress, he paused. Waiting for her permission.

Savannah nodded once, breathless.

Gently, reverently, Jamie slid the fabric upward, baring her inch by inch to the soft golden glow of the room. He knelt before her, his hands smoothing up her thighs, his mouth following the reverent trail of his touch.

Savannah gasped as his lips found the inside of her knee — a kiss so tender it felt like a vow. He kissed his way higher — slow, unhurried — worshipping her with the kind of aching devotion that made her heart splinter. At her hip, he nuzzled her skin, breathing her in like something sacred. And when he finally reached the core of her, he pressed a single kiss there — soft, reverent — as if praying.

Savannah whimpered, her hands threading through his hair, her body arching toward him instinctively.

Jamie murmured her name against her skin — a broken benediction — before he began to truly worship her. His mouth was gentle at first, coaxing pleasure from her with the slow patience of a man who had all the time in the world. He licked and kissed her with devastating tenderness, savoring every gasp, every tremor he drew from her body. His hands anchored her hips carefully, grounding her against the dizzying rush of sensation.

Every flick of his tongue, every press of his lips, was a love letter written directly against her skin — a promise, an apology, a prayer.

Savannah cried out softly, her thighs trembling around his shoulders, her fingers tightening in his hair.

Jamie didn't stop. Didn't rush. He worshiped her like a man making penance, like she was the only salvation left to him.

And when Savannah shattered — body arching, hands clinging to him like a lifeline — he held her through it, his mouth coaxing her through wave after wave until she sobbed his name into the heavy dark. She clung to him as he brought her to the brink over and over, until her body ached, until her heart could hold no more.

Only then did he lift his head, his face flushed, his mouth glistening, his eyes burning with a devotion so fierce it took her breath away. He rose slowly, gathering her into his arms, carrying her to the bed as if she weighed nothing at all. There, he wrapped himself around her, murmuring soft, cracked words into her hair — words of love, of devotion, of promises meant to be kept.

And Savannah wept — not from sorrow, but from

the unbearable beauty of being loved so completely. When finally they lay together, tangled and trembling, it was not brokenness she felt. It was completeness. She ran her fingers gently through his hair as he lay pressed against her, his breath slow and ragged against her skin.

"I have never felt anything so perfect," she whispered against his temple.

Jamie kissed her shoulder, silent, overwhelmed.

Later, as they lay wrapped around each other, the last candle guttering low, Savannah tilted his face toward hers. "I always dreamed of children," she said softly. "Of building a family."

Jamie's face crumpled, a silent apology already in his eyes. "I know," he whispered. "And I can't—"

She pressed her finger to his lips. "Then we'll make a family another way. Adoption. Fostering. Whatever we choose."

For a moment, something like hope sparked in Jamie's gaze. But it dimmed as quickly as it came. "Who would want to bring a child into this family?" he said, bitter.

Savannah held his face between her palms. "We aren't them," she said fiercely. "We are something new. Something they can never control."

Jamie closed his eyes, breathing her in like salvation.

Morning crept into the house on silent feet, casting long beams of pale gold across the worn hardwood floors. Savannah stirred awake, her body curled protectively around Jamie's.

For a moment, she simply lay there — listening to the soft rasp of his breathing, feeling the steady thump of his heartbeat beneath her palm. The air between them was warm, heavy with the scent of rain and crushed gardenias lingering on his skin.

The world outside had not changed — the mist still clung to the trees, the city still groaned and growled beyond their walls. But inside this fragile circle of their bodies, something had shifted. Something had been reclaimed.

Jamie woke slowly, blinking against the soft

morning light.

They stayed like that for a long time — holding, rocking, breathing. No demands. No expectations. Just the slow, trembling weaving of trust.

At last, Savannah pulled back slightly to cup his face between her hands. "Today," she said, her voice fierce and trembling, "we begin again." "No more Sinclair promises. No more bloodlines. No more veils and lies." "Just you and me."

Jamie nodded, his hand covering hers, grounding himself in her touch. "I swear it," he said, his voice breaking. "I swear it on everything that's real."

Savannah leaned forward and pressed her forehead to his, closing her eyes. They breathed each other in — slow, deliberate, sacred.

Later, wrapped in simple clothes and simple hopes, they stood side by side on the front porch.

Jamie carried a small box in his hands — the last remnants of the Handler legacy he had been born into. Old contracts. Letters. Trinkets meant to bind loyalty and fear. Savannah struck the match herself — a single flare of orange against the gray morning. Together, they set the box alight, watching the flames eat the past until only ash remained. Jamie's hand found hers. Fingers twining. No chains. No handlers. No fate but the one they chose together.

Inside their house, the shadows still whispered behind mirrors. The air still shifted strangely when the windows creaked open. And in the corners of old dreams, the hands behind the veil still wove.

But Savannah no longer feared them. Because she had chosen to see them. Because she had chosen to fight. Because she had chosen love — flawed, scarred, trembling — but hers. Completely hers.

She smiled. She was not naïve anymore. She was not a pawn anymore. She was a woman who had stared into the deepest shadow of her heart — and chosen to stay. To build. To love anyway.

Beside her, Jamie squeezed her hand tighter. The

future was unwritten. But for the first time in her life, Savannah knew: Whatever waited in the dark, whatever battles lay ahead — They would face it together.

A memory stirred — the whisper of old pages, the faded ink of her grandmother's journal. Savannah heard the words as clearly as if they were spoken aloud: "Beware the hands behind the veil, child. They weave what the heart cannot see. And what they weave, they mean to bind."

She closed her eyes and held Jamie tighter, praying that love would be enough for the battles still to come. But deep in her heart, Savannah knew the truth. It's not over, she thought, Not yet.

ABOUT THE AUTHOR

 Veronica R. Johnson writes stories that slip between shadow and light, weaving together fierce heroines, wounded heroes, and the magic found in the quietest corners of the world. Inspired by old myths, Southern folklore, and the strength of survivors, her books explore the deep ache of love, hope, and resilience against impossible odds. She believes every broken heart can still find a home. When she's not writing, Veronica enjoys rainy mornings, vintage bookstores, and finding secret gardens in unexpected places. This is her debut novel, but certainly not her last.